THE MERCIFUL EYE
STORIES
FROM THE MIDDLE AGES

THE MERCIFUL EYE
STORIES
FROM THE MIDDLE AGES

Christine Farenhorst

CF4•K

10 9 8 7 6 5 4 3 2 1

The Merciful Eye
© Christine Farenhorst 2010
ISBN 978-1-84550-562-2

Published by Christian Focus Publications
Geanies House, Fearn, Tain, Ross-shire,
IV20 1TW, Scotland, UK.
www.christianfocus.com

Cover design: Alister MacInnes
Printed and bound by Norhaven AS, Denmark

**Although a number of the stories are based on historical
events, all the main characters in the stories are fictitious.**

Contents

FOR A MOMENT

The Venerable Bede, (673-735), an English monk, scholar and church historian, tells us of the argument of a heathen thane, a chief, to persuade his king and his fellow country men, to study the Bible. His argument ran thus:

The present life of man, O King, may be likened to what often happens when thou art sitting at supper with thy thanes and nobles in winter-time. A fire blazes in the hearth and warms the chamber; outside rages a storm of wind and snow; a sparrow flies in at one door of thy hall, and quickly passes out at the other.

For a moment and while it is within, it is unharmed by the wintry blast, but this brief season of happiness is over when it returns to that wintry blast whence it came, and vanishes from thy sight.

Such is the brief life of man: we know not what went before it, and we are utterly ignorant as to what shall follow it. If, therefore, this new doctrine contains anything more certain, it justly deserves to be followed.

The lives of men are, indeed, short and it is a wise course of action to study the words of wisdom and truth contained in Scripture. Moses, in Psalm 90, ponders the brevity and uncertainly of life with great depth of feeling. It is a Psalm often read at open grave sides, and plumbs the emotions of the soul.

For all our days are passed away in thy wrath: we spend our years as a tale that is told. The days of our years are threescore years and ten; and if by reason of strength they be fourscore years, yet is their strength labour and sorrow; for it is soon cut off, and we fly away. (Psalm 90:9-10 KJV).

And after we fly away, what then?

It is my prayer that the stories contained in this book will provide food for thought with regard to what is important in life and to what is the purpose of our brief sojourn here on earth. For we travel from time to eternity.

Remember your leaders, those who spoke to you the word of God. Consider the outcome of their way of life, and imitate their faith.
(Hebrews 13:7)

Dedicated to my father, Louis Praamsma, (1910-1984): a wonderful leader who loved church history, who continually preached the Word of God, and whose faith was without compromise.

*It is easier for a camel
to go through the eye of a needle,
than for a rich person
to enter the kingdom of God.*
(Matthew 19:24)

The Merciful Eye

If wealth were to be counted in the beauty of nature and in the abundance of spring blossoms, then indeed Jacques Dalierre, more skin than bones, was a rich, little fellow. For cherry trees made the air sweet around him with their heavy boughs and magnificent, purple clusters of lilacs surrounded his village like a snug and most comfortable glove.

Besides that, there were many white poplars, ash trees and laurel groves where wood pigeons cooed. Oftentimes cuckoos also murmured softly in the wooded areas and fields; they murmured with long pauses, but regularly as clockwork. And those spring days when it rained, all the air was filled with a delightful aroma of growing things, of purity and peace.

Small Jacques Dalierre lived in the small village of St-Maurice in Aunis, France. Its gentle landscape with sloping hills and pristine beauty belied the fact that rampant poverty also lived here – a poverty where chestnuts, potatoes and wheat broth were the staple diet of most and a poverty where even cabbage soup was deemed a luxury.

Jacques and his four older brothers often went to bed hungry. Paul Dalierre, Jacques' father, was a simple peasant and it seemed that his five sons were destined to be simple peasants as well, were it not for a few moments in time, predestined from eternity, which drastically changed this lot for Jacques.

All of four years old, Jacques had wandered close to the vineyard of the Duc de Palons. A fine row of cypresses lined the south side of the vineyard and Jacques sat himself down next to one. Then, because it was a warm day and past noon, he fell asleep against the trunk. The boy was little and as thin as a bean pole, blending like a chameleon into the tree with his thin, tanned body. He woke much later to the sound of whispers, whispers discussing the murder of the Duc's steward.

The boy, who was sharp and quick-witted, first stayed quiet, rigid with fear lest the miscreants should discover him behind the tree. Yet he had enough courage to eventually peek around the trunk to discern who the plotters were and afterwards, when the men had left, to run like the wind on his four-year-old feet to the chateau. Able to relate to the steward what he had overheard, as well as naming the culprits, it was decided to catch the two villains in the act. This worked amazingly well and after the fellows confessed, the Duc de Palons was so pleased with the child that he took Jacques away from his parents' home to have the boy educated at the chateau alongside his own son.

Paul Dalierre was only too glad to have Jacques' future taken care of, for the Duc de Palons had promised that the boy should be prepared for the priesthood. So instead of chestnuts, potatoes, wheat broth and cabbage soup, the child was fed Latin letters. However, although he enjoyed the taste of this dish, Jacques became more and more convinced, as he grew older, that he had no stomach for the priesthood. It was not that he hated the church. Indeed, he was quite apathetic to the Roman Catholic faith. No, it was more that he desired to become rich and to be in control of his own affairs without having to wear a restraining black frock which might call him to account.

One of the newest of trades, and a very popular one, was that of printing. Many young men, not desirous of working as blacksmith, tailor, cooper or saddle maker, sought to become printers' apprentices. It seemed to Jacques, who was fascinated by letters, that this livelihood was much more desirable than the cowl. Consequently, he ran away from the monastery in which the Duc de Palons had placed him. Just prior to his thirteenth birthday Jacques arrived in Paris, hiring himself out with but little difficulty to Maurice Caval, a book printer.

Now it must be understood that printing, in the early fifteen hundreds, required a considerable investment. If one apprenticed to a book printer, five years of hard work were obligatory before an apprentice could attain the state of journeyman. And then it was highly unlikely, unless one was heir to a fortune, that one could open a workshop of his own. A book had to be printed, illustrated and bound. This process required paper, a press, type, engraved wood and binding materials. On top of this there must be space to work and hired help to engage for no one could run a printing shop on his own. Five or six apprentices and journeymen were needed for a small printing shop running only one press. Many more were needed for a shop with more than one press.

After working for Monsieur Caval for only a few months, it became Jacques' burning ambition to own a printing shop. He worked hard, pleased his employer and, in due time, became a journeyman. Considering his options, Jacques decided to stay with Monsieur Caval and to save his salary, a salary supplemented amply by the French crown, (which favoured the lucrative printing business since it was good for the French economy), and to begin courting Anna Maria, Monsieur Caval's oldest daughter.

Monsieur Caval, a widower, had no sons. His two daughters were Anna Maria and Aymee. Anna Maria had a wealth of reddish-brown hair, was small in stature and spoke in a refined and flirtatious manner. With the air of a charming coquette, she appealed to Jacques. But it was not her feminine wiles which captured his heart. It was her inheritance.

Anna Maria, not immune to the compliments and attentions of the hard-working journeyman, returned Jacques' attentions. Her father as well was not blind to the lad's good points and highly favoured the courtship. The young man knew how to work the press and how to print paper admirably. He had also mastered the skills of compositor; that is, he knew how to make the press roll, how to compose and collect characters into words, lines and pages. Monsieur Caval knew a good man when he saw one and he was not loath to keep these skills close at hand. For this reason Jacques, when he was but twenty years old, wed Anna Maria Caval with the hearty approval of her father.

In spite of this approval, however, it was stipulated by Maurice Caval that the young journeyman take a pledge before marrying his daughter. It was agreed upon, albeit reluctantly by Jacques, that all of the inheritance, that is to say the entire print shop, should go, upon the death of Maurice Caval, to Anna and her heirs. But although Jacques agreed to this, he quietly thought to himself that Maurice Caval could not live forever and what happened afterwards, well, that would not be Maurice Caval's concern anymore.

The wedding day dawned, bright and promising. Birds sang and Jacques whistled as he dressed for the nuptials. After he and the coy Anna Maria had taken the public pledge before witnesses at the church door, they entered the church to hear nuptial mass.

'Do you, Jacques Dalierre, agree to take Anna Maria Caval for your lawful wedded wife, to have and to hold before all others?'

Jacques readily answered that he did. Likewise Anna, being asked if she consented, nodded, bouncing her pretty reddish curls and enunciating in a clear voice that she would have and hold Jacques Dalierre before all others. After this, Jacques received Anna from the hand of one of the witnesses.

'I, Jacques Dalierre,' he promised for the second time, 'take thee, Anna Maria Caval, for my lawful wife, to have and to hold all the days of my life.'

Then, taking a ring which had been blessed by the priest from the priest's hand, he espoused Anna.

'With this ring I thee wed, with my body and goods I thee honour.'

As soon as the mass had been solemnized, Jacques led Anna, her father, her sister and all his fellow workers, away from the church back to the rooms he had rented above the printing shop. The company drank wine, ate bread and cheese and made merry for a while until Monsieur Caval remarked soberly that it was time to return to work. That evening, instead of sleeping on the small cot by the printing press, Jacques made his way upstairs to the family rooms and he was glad that he was married.

There was not any pretence on the part of either Jacques or Anna about being madly in love with one another. Jacques' main interest was in the printing business and Anna's primary concern was having a handsome husband who would provide for her even as her father had always provided. But even though the marriage was an arrangement of sorts, it was not a sad affair. Anna kept Jacques happy by entertaining him in the evenings with small anecdotes; she coddled him by cooking up special dishes; and she laughed a great deal. He was quite satisfied.

It was a busy life. Jacques worked hard. He printed great Bibles, and the works of doctors of the Church, such as Jerome, Augustine, Chrysostom and others. Many lectures on civil and canon law and other works which were long in labour and great in cost, were run through the press. Nations who valued letters highly came to Paris, to obtain the works printed there. It was the year of our Lord 1523 and what a golden decade it was for France with regard to printing. Not one of these years passed without foreigners bringing into France a million in gold. The printers profited. Jacques profited and he hoarded his savings in a small niche in the wall of the bedroom. And his pile of gold coins grew steadily as did his trust in them.

Ten years following Jacques' marriage to Anna, she bore a living child. She had born four dead. It was a little girl child who was baptized immediately by the midwife as she believed this would ensure the child's small soul a place in heaven. The midwife was paid and then, when all seemed good and well, Anna haemorrhaged and died, the baby following her to the grave two days later. Jacques grieved. He had come to be fond of Anna, but it was the inheritance which he grieved for the most. Consequently, in the months that followed Anna's death, he began his courtship of Aymee - Aymee, the younger sister who had never married.

Aymee was not as well-favoured physically as Anna had been. Shy, slightly dowdy in appearance, she did not initially respond to Jacques' amorous advances but hid away in her room. Monsieur Caval, however, was not averse to the alliance of his second daughter to the head journeyman and he spoke severely to her. Dutifully Aymee obeyed her father's wishes but it was not a glad, or even a slightly smiling bride whom Jacques wed that following spring. The same nuptial agreements held and all of the inheritance was now pledged to Aymee and her heirs.

Aymee's temperament differed greatly from that of Anna. Although she prepared Jacques' meals, stitched his clothes when these needed mending, and kept their rooms clean, she never voluntarily engaged him in conversation. Indeed, it seemed at times that she only tolerated him. Jacques, who had not truly loved Anna Maria, now felt his heart strangely touched. He sought to please his new bride, to seek her approbation in his hard work. But although not unfriendly towards her new husband, Aymee retained a noncommittal attitude towards him. She regularly walked the streets, roaming about, especially when travelling Franciscans, Augustinians and secular priests were said to be in the market place. But when he asked her what she had seen or what she had done during the day, she remained quiet to the point of morose although she listened politely to Jacques' attempts at conversation.

Aymee especially seemed to grieve for her sister Anna, whom she had loved very much, and Jacques reasoned within himself that when her grief had run its course, she would naturally turn her attention to the living, to himself.

On St. Mark's Day, some six months after her marriage to Jacques, Aymee heard a Dominican preach on a street corner.

'What does it mean to believe in Jesus?' the friar called out.

Aymee, who was on her way to market, stopped. A great many other people stopped as well.

'Is it to believe that He is both God and man; that He was crucified and died for us; that He descended into hell, ascended into heaven, and is seated at the right hand of God; and that He will come to judge all mankind?'

There were all sorts of folks crowded around Aymee onto the small corner where they were standing - children, holding onto their mothers' hands, peasants with baskets, old women out for a stroll and several well-born gentry. No one responded to the Dominican. But they stood quietly, waiting to hear how he would answer his own questions.

'People of Paris, what is faith? Or, more personally put – what is your faith?'

Again no one answered and the friar continued.

'I'll tell you what it should be!! Faith should be that you believe firmly and hope securely that, because the Son of God became man, you, although nothing but a poor creature, can participate in divine perfection. Because Jesus suffered a painful death, your sins will be forgiven. Because He descended into hell, the devil will have no power over you. Because He rose again, one day we will also rise again. Because He went to heaven, Paradise is opened to us and we will follow Him. In short, faith in Jesus is to believe that we will never have any part in Paradise except by virtue of that faith ...'

Aymee pushed her way through the people and walked on without waiting to hear how the Dominican continued to define faith. She was troubled. His words had rung wonderfully sweet in her ears but it was not what the local priest constantly told her. That is to say, it was not what she had been brought up to believe. Scrupulously, and without fail, she had been taught to give total devotion to Mary, the mother of Jesus. She had been conditioned to pluck endlessly at her beads while quietly evoking the Virgin and she had been told to endlessly intone litanies. It irritated Jacques to no end.

'Hail, Star of the Sea, Window of Heaven, Tower of David, Rose Without a Thorn, intercede for me; Lily of the Valleys, Fountain, Mirror without Blemish, Perfumed Nard, protect me and let not Anna suffer in purgatory.'

Aymee wore her knees to scabs at the feet of the life size statues of Mary at the many shrines around Paris. She could not bear the thought of the laughing and beautiful Anna suffering in purgatory and shuddered to think of her own soul. Weeping openly at confession, she was often so distraught that finally Father Lapin, her confessor, urged her to pray at the corner of Rue St. Antoine.

'Years ago some wicked person decapitated the stone heads of both the Virgin and the Child. But our good King Francis the First, praise his name, was so angry that he ordered religious processions all over Paris.'

He paused for a moment in his enthusiasm, breathing loudly through the grille that separated him from Aymee. He was a short priest and, unlike many fellow priests, thin. He fasted often and even now genuinely desired to help Aymee come to grips with her fear of purgatory.

'You must go to Rue St. Antoine,' he repeated, 'for the silver statue that King Francis had made of the Blessed Virgin is reputed to be beautiful.'

'This statue of the Blessed Mary can forgive sins for the dead?'

Aymee whispered the question hopefully. Father Lapin considered a moment before he answered.

'It is a wooden statue but overlaid with a silver casing. And King Francis placed it in the shrine with his own royal hands. Surely God was pleased that a king should place such a statue in a shrine with his own hands.'

Aymee peered at him earnestly.

'But I seek the forgiveness of my sister's sins, father. For you know, as I told you before, that she was not shriven before she died.'

'Ah!!'

Father Lapin sighed long and hard. He was unsure about Anna's state himself but he was truly fond of Aymee, who often prayed in his chapel, was generous in her giving and sincere in her devotions.

'I heard a priest say last week,' Aymee continued softly, 'that if we believe in Jesus and in His death, our sins ...' She hesitated and then continued shyly, ' our sins will be forgiven ... will be forgiven because we believe this.'

'No, no, no, child!! These are the ramblings of the Lutherans - of the miserable Protestants. They are wrong and wicked and deceive many women like yourself. We must work very hard to overcome our sins. There are many things to do ... many things ...'

He stopped his rather vehement discourse. Aymee blinked back tears. Father Lapin saw it and felt compassion.

'You must go to Rue St. Antoine, child. But not to the silver statue. No, not to that one. There is actually an even better one which will suit all your needs and give you much comfort. Go to the church opposite the shrine. It is there that they took the mutilated statue without the head and this statue is reported to be performing miracles.'

Aymee took Father Lapin's advice and walked to Rue St. Antoine the next day. It was not difficult to locate the church opposite the silver statue. It was a sizeable structure and when she entered a full service was in process. The priest, mounted on a high pulpit, was in the act of showing something to the people below. He wore red gloves and waved about a cloth, dark and sombre with some bright needlework wrought on it. The people below him cried out and prostrated themselves. Aymee, who knelt down in the last pew, looked up at it in wonder. An old woman, kneeling next to her, whispered that the cloth the priest held was the handkerchief of St. Veronica and that it was known to possess great powers.

'Has it the power to forgive sins?' Aymee asked hopefully.

'I do not know,' the old woman answered. 'But I am sure that if you light candles and put money into the coffers beneath, it is as much as anyone can do for the forgiveness of sins.'

Aymee stayed for a long time in the church even after all the others had left. She had with her thirty gold coins which she had taken out of the niche in the bedroom wall. Jacques never made a secret of the fact that he was saving the money and often counted it out to her upon their bed. She had no qualms about taking the money reasoning to herself that since Anna had been married to Jacques he ought to pay for her salvation. Thirty was the number of years Anna had lived on earth and surely an equal amount of gold coins would go a long way to rescuing her from purgatory.

'Can I help you, daughter?'

Aymee looked up from her prayers and saw the hawkish, lean face of a young priest.

'I've come to pray,' she faltered.

'And what do you pray for?'

'My sister ... she died ... and she was not shriven. Father Lapin, my priest, he thought that perhaps I could pray in front of the statue of the Virgin – the statue which has no head ...'

'Ah.'

The priest looked thoughtful.

'It is a statue kept in a side room. We treasure it and keep it most guardedly.'

'I would very much like to pray to it.'

The priest did not answer but waited. Anna continued.

'I've brought some money ... gold coins ... I thought that this would help shorten her stay in purgatory ...?'

The priest took her arm, helping her rise from her kneeling position.

'This is a good and kind thought. Perhaps I can persuade Father Etienne to write you an indulgence.'

'An indulgence?'

'Yes. This is a paper which you can buy and it can remit sins committed here on earth.'

'For my sister?'

'Yes, for your sister if you so wish.'

While he was talking, the priest led Aymee down the aisle towards the entrance of the church. At the entrance they turned to the right, into a narthex. Standing still by a half-open door, the priest took her hand, and spoke again.

'You may enter this room. It contains the head of St. Bartimaeus. It is not as efficacious as the broken Virgin but if you pray to this saint, it will certainly do some good. I will see if you are to be permitted to see the statue of Our Lady.'

Letting go of her hand, the priest smiled at her and continued walking down the hall. Hesitantly Aymee pushed the door open further and stepped inside. It was dark in the room. A dais of sorts, about four and a half feet high, stood in the centre of the room. A box with a heavy iron grating before it was on the dais and several candles were lit before the grating.

Cautiously Aymee made her way towards the dais. Her heart beat loudly and she could not but be fearful of seeing a head - a head without a body. She had been prepared for a statue without a head but this was not the same. The candles glowed eerily and her footsteps faltered. She had to bend down somewhat to peer through the grating into the box. The face of a lifeless wax countenance stared at her. It had a forked beard, reddish tinted cheeks and a papal mitre. The eyes were light green and glassy, the skin shiny and repulsive. Aymee swallowed and tearing her gaze away began an 'Ave Maria'. But she could not formulate her words properly. Repelled by the head, she questioned, for the first time in her life, whether or not she was sane in her worship. The candles flickered and a choking sensation took hold of her. Walking backwards, she bumped into the door. Nervously she turned, edging her way out. Not thinking about where she was going, she continued down the hallway for a few minutes, until she heard voices coming from behind a closed door.

'But I don't know how much money she has.'

It was the voice of the priest who had told her to wait. Another voice, much deeper than his, answered.

'It is proper, brother Parvant, to ascertain sums before disturbing me. You are well aware of that.'

'Yes, yes. But I'm certain the girl, if spoken to properly, will come back – come back with money. And she will, no doubt, always bring something. She was dressed well, spoke in a refined manner, and I'm certain that ...'

Aymee froze in her spot. Her eyes were riveted on the door. Then she turned and bolted back down the hall. The front door of the church was open and the street beyond seemed infinitely cleaner and sweeter than the confines of the sanctuary. She ran out, not looking to the right or to the left. There was a deadness, an emptiness in her. Within the few moments that she had heard that small conversation idols had toppled; within seconds, shrines had collapsed. Aymee felt betrayed and alone. Weeping, she returned to her home above the printing shop.

Jacques was puzzled that evening. He had found Aymee huddled into a small ball on their bed. She had wept when he touched her but was unable to give him an account of what had happened to her. He sat on the edge of the bed and stroked her shoulder. Her long gown trailed onto the floor and he fingered its woollen softness.

Finally, after sitting by her for more than an hour with no results, he stood up. Stretching and yawning, his belly rumbling for a supper that had never materialized, he decided to count his savings. Upon hearing him fumbling with the hiding place which hid his savings, Aymee suddenly sat up. Her cheeks puffy with weeping, her hair tousled and her skirts awry, she looked the epitome of misery.

'Here,' she said, reaching into the left pocket of her gown, 'Here's what you will be wanting. You count and count, but what for?'

She flung the gold coins she had taken from his niche onto the floor. They clattered and clinked and rolled about the wooden floor.

'Where did you get ...' Jacques began and then knelt down to carefully retrieve the money.

Aymee laughed but ended with weeping again.

'From your treasure box there in the wall,' she said, 'I took it from your savings.'

Jacques was perplexed. Aymee was not a frivolous creature. She never asked for material, for trinkets, for brooches or any such things.

'Why,' he questioned slowly, 'Why did you take my money? Did you need something?'

She answered in a tremulous voice.

'What do you know of need? You work ... you always work for the money. But someday ... someday you will die ...'

She stopped short and tears ran down her face again. It was to Jacques' credit that he left the little pile of coins he had gathered and went over to the bed again.

'But we will not die today, love. Besides, what has the money got to do with dying?'

He sat down next to his wife, put his arm about her and felt immensely rewarded when she lay her head on his shoulder, all the while shuddering with inward emotion.

'There, there,' he comforted, 'perhaps you are in the family way ... I think ...'

But Aymee violently shook her head.

'No, I am not! I am not with child!'

'Well,' he responded, quite at a loss as to what could be the cause of all her turmoil, 'that is no matter. But I wish you would tell me what causes you such pain.'

Aymee sat up straight again and looked down at the coverlet on the bed.

'I think,' she said, 'that I do not believe any more ...'

Now it was Jacques' turn to laugh.

'Not believe,' he answered, 'well, that is no cause for concern. I know very few who do and many who say they do but do not really.'

'But I want to believe,' Aymee desperately retorted, 'I must believe, don't you see. I ... I ...'

And she fell to weeping again with such agonizing sobs that Jacques knew not what to do. He patted her shoulder again and after a long while, she fell asleep.

With Aymee sleeping on the bed, Jacques gathered the scattered coins and, putting them in a small heap, counted them. Thirty there were – an odd number. Glancing over at the prostrate form of his wife, he could not fathom why she was so distraught. Believe? He believed little enough himself. To be sure, he rarely thought on things pertaining to faith. But did these things really matter? What mattered was to work hard, to earn money and to save enough to buy a printing shop. That is to say, perhaps Maurice Caval would soften and pass this shop on to himself, the admirable son-in-law.

Early the next day, when Jacques got up, Aymee was still asleep. She had not stirred all night and he left quietly, reasoning that sleep would probably put all things into proper perspective with her. But when he checked in at noon, he was disturbed to find her in a chair, simply staring at her rosary. All she would say to him were the words, 'I must believe. I cannot believe nothing. It does not work.'

It was by chance, but such a thing is not, that the shop was printing a pamphlet for a merchant reported to be of the Huguenot cause. It was a bit risky to be printing for those of that persuasion, but the merchant was wealthy and money was after all money. So Maurice Caval reasoned and Jacques agreed wholeheartedly. Jacques was not overly involved in the politics of religion but that day, as the words formed lines and the lines became pages, he thought that perhaps a new way of thinking might not be bad for Aymee. Perhaps if he took a copy of the pamphlet up to her, she might be shaken out of her lethargy. And so it was that, armed with several pages of Huguenot writing as well as some bread, cheese and wine which he had bought, that he returned to his rooms early that evening.

Aymee was still sitting in the chair. She was pale, had not combed her hair and did not move as he entered. He wondered, as he had often done in the past months, at his feelings for the girl. She was, after all, no beauty, and neither did she display any of the sometimes blatant charms which her sister had so openly flouted. But he could not deny the fact that he loved this woman. It was a mystery to him. He walked over to her chair and knelt down.

'I've brought you some food, Aymee. Let's eat a bit and then I'll read you something we printed today. Perhaps it will make you feel better.'

She did not stir and he sighed. Seating himself on the bed, he took a bite of the bread and a drink of the wine. Laying the paper on his lap, he began to read in the rapidly dimming light of dusk. At first Aymee did not respond at all and Jacques' voice droned on, seemingly only to himself. But at length she moved and her eyes became riveted on his face. Jacques stopped but she motioned that he continue. He had not really paid any attention himself to the words which he had been reading. But now he began listening to himself.

'... The mark of a true Gospel is given by our Lord and Saviour Himself. True Gospel promotes the glory, not of men, but of God as we read in John 7:18 and 8:50. Men everywhere are in serious error if they think that there can be miraculous works, works which are used for other purposes than to magnify the name of God!

'It is important to remember that Satan also works miracles, which, although they are tricks and not miracles, can still delude the ignorant and unwary. Magicians and enchanters as well, are famous for miracles in which those wicked people try to shake the faith of the simple-minded. But the Lord warned us against those wonder-workers when He said in Matthew 24:24 that false prophets would arise, who, by lying signs and wonders would, if it were possible, deceive the very elect. Paul, in 2 Thessalonians 2:9 also said that the reign of the antichrist would be with all power, and signs, and lying wonders.'

Jacques stopped for breath. He did not understand why this should so take Aymee's complete concentration.

'I was in a church yesterday,' Aymee began.

She looked past him at the wall and seemed almost not to note that he was there.

'I was taken to see the head of a saint. It was gruesome and horrible and filthy and I went away from the room in which it was. By chance, as I walked down the hallway, I overheard a priest, the same priest who had taken me to see the relic, say some things.'

She stopped and Jacques prodded her.

'What did he say, Aymee?'

She looked at him directly now.

'He was speaking to another priest, I suppose. I did not see him. He was in a room and I was in the hallway. They discussed money, the money that they supposed I had and how it would be feasible to have me return so that they would get me to bring more money. It was as common as a butcher discussing how to sell ham hocks!'

She looked down at her beads now, twisting them around her fingers. Then, suddenly, with a motion that frightened Jacques, she flung them at the wall. They broke and spilt and rolled onto the floor, even as the day before the gold coins had rolled. Aymee continued.

'And when I heard them speak, I knew in the fraction of a second that all my years of prayers, that all my faith in the saints, was nothing. And now my life is nothing!!'

She paused and turned her eyes to the paper Jacques was holding in his hands.

'But it is so strange that what you read to me now I feel to be true. Jacques, have you ever read the Bible? Have you ever studied the words of our Lord?'

Jacques shook his head.

'When I studied with the tutor when I was younger, it was always the classics he taught, saying that when I was put into a monastery, they would likely have me copying out the Scriptures for the rest of my life.'

He smiled at her suddenly. There was such a feeling in him of lightheartedness. For was he not talking to Aymee and was she not talking to him? What did it matter that it was about such a dry subject as the Bible? Eager to please her he continued.

'But should you want to read the Scriptures, I can obtain a copy and I can read it to you after I come up at night.'

She smiled back.

'Thank you, Jacques.'

And he was as pleased as if she had embraced him of her own free will.

They read together after that, every evening, that late summer and early fall of 1534. There was no one to guide them but Jacques did not mind that. Beginning with Genesis and working through the Old Testament, they read intimately night after night. It seemed as if Aymee could not get enough and after a time, because of her interest and discussion, Jacques was taking in the spirit of the books as well.

On the morning of 18th October, 1534, Paris awoke to find that its churches, public buildings and monuments had all been plastered with placards. Maurice Caval's printing shop had not been touched but nearby places of residence were covered with billboards. These notices reviled the mass; they made fun of fat priests; they derided prayers for the dead and they mocked transubstantiation. King Francis who had been at his palace in Blois, south-west of Paris, had travelled back to the capital. Inclined to be rather permissive with matters of religion, he was incensed to find a rude note tacked to the door of the Louvre as well as another tacked on the door of his private apartments. And if that were not enough, there was also a note under the pillow of his royal bed. His authority was obviously being mocked and a mocking of himself was one thing Francis could not abide. A wave of inquisitorial bigotry now began.

Jacques and Aymee were just beginning to understand the Scriptures. That is to say, Aymee's heart was at peace and she felt a new joy each morning as she anticipated the reading she would do that evening with Jacques. Jacques noted a change in Aymee's attitude towards him. She had become more affectionate, displayed sweetness in disposition and tried very hard to be a useful wife. Even her father, who usually was silent on marital matters, commented that Jacques must have done something to please his daughter, for he had never seen her so content. In the aftermath of the placard business, Father Lapin came to call on Aymee. He had not seen her at confession for weeks and was concerned that she might be ill. Aymee received him in her sitting room with great misgivings.

'Well, daughter, you are looking well.'

Aymee smiled. She felt well but was unsure as to what to say to Father Lapin. She was fond of him as she was sure that the priest had never intentionally deceived her.

'I have not seen you for a long time,' he continued.

She offered him a glass of wine but he waved his hand about.

'No, thank you.'

It was her that he had come to see. He had not come for refreshment. She coughed and wished that Jacques were with her. It was close to noon. Maybe he would be up early today for his lunch.

'Are you perhaps attending another church? Have you another priest who hears your confession?'

Father Lapin's thin face was anxious and he peered at her studiously.

'No, Father.'

'Why, then, child, have you not been to see me? Why have you not been to mass?'

'Well, I have not felt up to it.'

Aymee worded her sentence cautiously and a light suddenly broke upon the priest's face.

'Ah, you are perhaps a bit ill ... just a bit ...?'

He smiled and stood up.

'Say no more. Say no more. I understand such things and will look for you when you are perhaps a bit further along?'

Aymee did not reply. She did not understand the priest's meaning until it suddenly dawned on her that he thought she was expecting. She blushed.

'No, father, no. This is not ...'

But he was already at the door.

'I should have thought of this myself. Such a pious woman as yourself would not stay away for any other reason. I will pray for you daughter.'

And then he was gone.

She told Jacques and he laughed. Then they kissed for were they not man and wife and had they not but of late discovered that love was a gift of God.

'I would that it were true,' Aymee said at length.

'What?'

'That I were carrying your child.'

She spoke wistfully but he, remembering that her sister had died in childbed, shook his head.

'I have heard,' Jacques said, suddenly remembering something he had discovered that day, 'that there will be a meeting of Huguenots in Rue la Pladin this evening. There will be a pastor of that religion speaking. Would you like to go?'

'Yes.'

It was all that Aymee said, but she felt excitement and a tension mounting within her. When Monsieur Caval asked where they were going that evening, both Jacques and Aymee remained silent.

'Come, come,' he said, 'You never venture out at night so it must be something rather special.'

'We are off to a meeting, father,' Aymee said, and spontaneously kissed him on his cheek.

She was not given to much affection and the old man did not know what to think of it.

'What meeting?' he asked.

'Oh,' Jacques answered nonspecifically, 'a meeting with some friends.'

'Well, just remember that tomorrow comes all too soon and that you will have to be up early.'

They both nodded and left and the old man stared after them, and then, without putting on his cloak, followed them down the street.

It was but a small fellowship they found in the designated house on Rue la Pladin. About twelve people were already gathered, earnestly listening to a speaker. This man, soberly dressed in black hose and jacket, held a Bible in his right hand. Jacques and Aymee sat down, uncertain as to whether they should say anything or not. But several people smiled at them and the leader stopped for a moment to welcome them.

'My name is brother Rombard, and I trust that you will worship with us in peace.'

Aymee shifted on her chair. Her hand was hidden within Jacques' hand and he squeezed it softly. Brother Rombard continued speaking.

'As long as we are without Christ, beloved friends, and separated from Him, nothing which He suffered and did for the salvation of mankind is of the least benefit to us. To communicate to us the blessing of the Father, He must dwell in us. We must be clothed with Him.'

Aymee fingered her dress. To be clothed with Christ, to be completely covered by Him, this was a wonderful thought. If only Anna was still alive so that she could speak to her about this.

'Many of you,' brother Rombard said, 'are wealthy. I can tell by your dress and, indeed, by your hands, that a number of you are not accustomed to hard work. Wealth is a dangerous thing to have.'

He stopped and looked long and hard at all of them before adding his next sentence.

'To strive only for material riches in this life is foolish. Jesus Himself told His disciples that it would be hard for those who possess wealth to enter the kingdom of God.'

Jacques felt singled out. But what did the man know about him anyway?

'We must be sanctified by the Holy Spirit.'

Brother Rombard looked sincerely at the small company in front of him.

'That is, our souls must be washed in Christ's blood. It all comes down to this: that the Holy Spirit is the bond by which Christ effectually binds us to Himself. And how do we know that we have the Holy Spirit? By how we think, act and feel.

I said a moment ago that it is very difficult for those who have wealth to enter the kingdom of God. That is what Jesus said. When He said this the disciples were surprised. They had wrong ideas about prosperity - wrong ideas about wealth and health. They thought that if a man had riches, it meant that God was most certainly on his side.'

Aymee glanced about. It was a fact that most of the women in the room had flowing gowns, fur lined hems, and elaborate head wear. And the men wore expensive and well-cut tunics.

'What holds true for the rich, is true for us all, namely, that it is an extremely difficult thing to enter the kingdom of God. It is so difficult that for a rich man it can be, in a sense, almost impossible. Jesus Himself said: "It is easier for a camel to go through the eye of a needle than for a rich man to enter the kingdom of God."'

Brother Rombard smiled and they all smiled back at him, slightly uncomfortable.

'It is, of course, impossible for a camel to go through the eye of a needle. But it is easier for a camel to do this, than for a rich man to go to heaven.'

Jacques shifted and felt uneasy. He did not like this talk about money and wealth and inadvertently his thoughts went to the bag of money in the bedroom – the money he was saving so carefully; the coins he often counted with such delight.

'So can the rich not go to heaven? Well, beloved, no one can, in his own power work his way into the kingdom of God. This, you see, is impossible. The hold that wealth has on hearts makes this so. And who, I ask you, is free from the power that riches, or money, has over one's heart?'

There was a hush in the room. Jacques swallowed audibly.

'Who then can be saved? This is what the disciples asked Jesus and He answered: 'With men this is impossible but with

God all things are possible.' You see, dear friends, God has provided a way out. And what is that way? Well, you must recognize that by yourself you can do nothing - not one thing.'

Jacques thought of himself, toiling away in the printing room, working with the ink which dried almost as soon as it was applied. It was an art. He thought of himself composing and collecting characters, a formidable job. It was, as he had often said, a job which in a day could easily do the work of three or four thousand of the best scribes in the world.

'At every turn of your day,' and brother Rombard's voice grew more earnest and intense, 'you must depend upon God. In the beginning of the day, in the middle, and at the end - you must depend totally upon Him at all times. Because by yourself, and I repeat, by yourself, you can do nothing - not one thing. If you are to be saved, you must be born again through the Holy Spirit. Even when by God-given faith man reaches out to God, he must be enabled and supported every day, hour, minute and second by God's grace. Do you understand this? You must give up all to follow God. Whatever takes a higher place in your life than the sovereignty of God, stands in the way of your salvation.'

There was a small movement by the door and as heads turned, Aymee and Jacques were startled to see Monsieur Caval enter. Brother Rombard stopped his discourse.

'You are most welcome, sir,' he said, 'please find a place to sit in our midst.'

'No,' Monsieur Caval retorted, 'no, I have simply come to find my children. They must come home with me. This is a dangerous place, sir. A most dangerous place. Especially as the king smells heresy in this placard business.'

He stood uncertain for a moment and then walked into the room a bit further, his eyes searching all the while. Aymee gripped Jacques' hand. She had turned very pale.

'It is better we go,' he whispered to her, actually not averse to leaving, 'or he will cause a scene and then who knows what will happen?'

He stood up and pulled Aymee up with him. Maurice saw them and satisfied that they were coming, nevertheless, put in a parting gibe as he turned to walk out.

'All of you would do better to attend Mass.'

Outside they walked in silence for some time. Aymee sensed her father's disapproval and shivered. Eventually, Maurice began to shower them with his anger. He spoke in a low voice but it held much bitterness.

'You fools!! Do you think that I will tolerate this? You will ruin the business. You will put us all in jail. Do you not know lists have been compiled of clerks, of people who run bookstores, of those who shun the Mass, of ... of ...'

He spluttered in his rage and continued.

'Even the King's sister, Queen Marguerite of Navarre, is not beyond suspicion and has been summoned to Paris by her brother.'

Aymee pressed closer to Jacques and he put his arm about her as they walked.

'Father, we are simply looking for truth ... for ...,' she faltered as she spoke.

Maurice turned abruptly and slapped her soundly on the cheek.

'You ungrateful child!'

His voice rose and he was so agitated that he choked on his words. Jacques let go of Aymee, stepped forward, grabbed Maurice's arm and held it in a vice grip.

'Never do that again, sir!'

He spoke the words slowly and clearly. But the older man was not listening. Seemingly crumpling under Jacques' touch, his cheeks turned a livid red and he could not catch his breath. Aymee moved forward to support him, but he pushed her away, wheezing sharply.

'Help him, Jacques! Help him!'

Jacques was not sure what he should do. He had loosened his grip immediately when his father-in-law began to gasp for air. Unable to stand, Maurice fell to his knees. His eyes bulged out of his head. Aymee fell to her knees as well and tried to hold onto her father. But life ebbed out of him quickly and she could neither aid him nor fight the tide that swept him away.

'The truth ...' Maurice whispered, as he lay on the unswept street, 'I have never looked ... I have never looked for it ... and ... and now it finds me, I think.'

He shuddered and then lay still, his eyes staring out blankly.

Maurice had spoken the truth about one thing, and that was about the wave of arrests, trials and inquisitorial tortures which followed in the weeks after his death. Writers, printers and book-sellers were prosecuted right, left and centre. And some of them were burned alive. Many Reformed leaders were banished, executed or driven into exile. Jacques carried on the printing business. It was Aymee's now but she relinquished all care of it to him and put it in writing. It pleased him no end to be the master-printer, to be in charge, to collect the moneys due for printing pamphlets, books and treatises. They did not go back to Rue de Pladin and were somewhat more careful about reading the Scriptures. Actually there were evenings when Jacques did not come upstairs until it was time for bed and he would find Aymee asleep, weary with waiting for him. But the hoard of gold coins grew and grew, until the niche became almost too small to contain the wealth Jacques continued to put there.

Some two months after the death of Maurice, a public atonement took place. Francis the First, the king of France, convinced by his bishops that God had been offended by the placard business, arranged for a procession to take place in Paris. The entire contingent of priests and bishops of Paris, including Father Lapin, were involved. The clergy were all designated to carry some sort of relic, including the body of St. Genevieve and the head of Louis IX. Father Lapin came to see Aymee, asking her if she would walk behind him with a group of his parishioners, who would all be bare-footed. She told him 'no', and after a surreptitious glance at her belly, the priest left.

The procession was huge. A cavalcade of cardinals, archbishops, theologians, choirs, chaplains, Sorbonne University professors, scores and scores of bare-headed priests, and bare-footed Parisians, (some of whom had been assigned the dubious honour of carrying St. Genevieve's coffin and the casket containing Louis' head), were at the front. Behind this crowd followed archers, heralds, trumpeters, members of the royal family, torchbearers and those who carried a royal canopy displaying fleur de lis. Impressively, and quite by himself, Francis the First came next. He was on foot, bare-headed, carrying a virgin-white wax taper. Strolling a number of paces behind him, his monkey court paraded, as well as ambassadors, foreign dignitaries, the Parliament, guild-members and servants.

Never before had there been such a parade travelling so many of the roads throughout Paris. Jacques and Aymee, along with many others, watched from the sidelines. Groups of people passed and kept on passing. Weary at last, Aymee nudged Jacques indicating that she wanted to return home. He was not reluctant to go as he considered time away from the shop money. But just as they were about to turn into the crowd behind them, a man passing them in the procession caught Aymee's eye. It was the priest to whom she had spoken in the church on Rue de Antoine, the priest who had taken her to see the head of St. Bartimaeus. Half-fascinated, half-repulsed, Aymee stood and looked at him. And he recognized her. Sidling out of his position of clerics, he made his way towards them. Jacques, at Aymee's side, had no idea who the man was. Aymee felt both cold and nauseous under the man's calculating gaze. But she could not move.

'Sister, how good to see you here. Is it not a marvellous procession?'

Both Jacques and Aymee nodded, although Jacques was nonplussed that a priest should go out of his way to speak to them.

'You know my wife?'

'Indeed, I do. I met her after her sister's death and she rather disappeared on me.'

He stood solidly in front of them, holding a silver cross in his right hand. The crowd around them gaped at the ostentatious image, but Aymee looked at her shoes.

'So you must tell me why you left so suddenly.'

It all came back to her. The hungry voices as she had been standing in the hall, the deep and heartfelt knowledge that all she had been taught from childhood on was a lie and the fact that all these men had wanted was her money, not her salvation or that of her sister. She looked up and met the priest's eye steadily.

'I heard you speaking,' she said.

'Heard me speaking?'

'Yes.'

Then Aymee turned away completely and began pushing her way through the crowd. Jacques looked at the priest and shrugged. Then he followed his wife.

That night, six Reformed pastors were burned at the stake. Their punishment for teaching the Bible to their congregations was heightened by the estrapade, which consisted in first lowering them into the fire, then lifting them out for a moment to exhort them to recant. They did not recant, a fact which Martel, one of the journeymen at the shop, told Jacques about in great detail. Jacques did not pass this information on to Aymee and he stopped bringing the Bible upstairs for reading. Aymee had become very quiet again and often seemed not to note when he returned from work. One evening, coming upstairs rather early, he did not find her at all. Her surcoat was gone and he had no idea where she was.

Taking his cloak, he went downstairs and headed up the street. There were a number of people about and they all seemed to be heading towards the market square. Perhaps, he reasoned within himself, there is something going on there which Aymee knew about and she neglected to tell me. Perhaps she has gone there. He fell in with a group of people heading in the direction for the square and could tell from a distance that a pile of faggots had been prepared for a burning. He hesitated. He did not like to be confronted thus again with the new religion. It had all been very well to sit in his room and read together with Aymee, but to display one's faith so openly, to die for it, seemed to him very foolish. But he found it difficult to turn back. There were many more people about now that he was close to the square and he was rapidly being carried along, albeit reluctantly, to the place of execution.

A number of loudmouths pointed with a terrible degree of cruelty to the condemned man. He was not very old, Jacques saw. And there was something familiar about the man. In spite of himself, he moved closer and yet closer still. It was at this point that the condemned man began to offer up a prayer for the conversion of his persecutors. As he stood by the stake, and while the faggots were being kindled, his earnest voice rang out over the crowd. His voice rang familiar. Jacques felt both cold and uncomfortable. Then the man's eyes met his own. By this time he had reached the front row. With a shock he now saw that the condemned man was brother

Rombard, the speaker at Rue de Pladin. Fixing his eye on Jacques, brother Rombard looked at him steadily and Jacques, eyes quailed before that gaze. And even though the man was silent for a moment, the very faggots seemed to scream out. 'It is easier for a camel to go through the eye of a needle than for a rich man to enter the kingdom of heaven.'

The flames blazed about the martyr and still his voice rang out and still his eye did not turn away from Jacques.

'Father, forgive them for they know not what they do.'

Brother Rombard's clothes were burning now and his arms on fire but still his voice rang out and still his gaze stayed on Jacques.

'Father, into your hands I commend my spirit.'

And Jacques fled, weeping as he went, pushing his way through the crowd, tripping in his haste, running back to the shop. And it was dark outside.

Aymee was back in the room when he returned. She did not, as she had been doing of late, ignore his entrance, but looked up and smiled.

'Jacques, I went back.'

'What?'

He was drained and felt as if all had been taken from him. Walking over to the wall, he took out the stone which covered the niche. Trembling all over, he removed the bag and walked over to the bed. He emptied it out and began counting.

'One, two, three gold coins. Four, five ...'

How they glittered and shone. His hands shook and he resisted the urge to weep again.

'Jacques, I went back to Rue de Pladin.'

'It is no good. They burned brother Rombard tonight.'

'I know. I heard.'

'How did you hear?'

'From some of the others who were there. They are thinking of leaving for Geneva, as a group. There is a guide.'

'Geneva?' he replied stupidly.

'Yes, or Navarre. There are groups of people who feel that congregations can be set up in Navarre. It is safer there - more tolerant of this new faith.'

'You want to leave here?'

She got up and moved behind him, putting her hands on his shoulders.

'Yes, I want to leave. I want to learn more about Jesus, about life after death, about why I am living and I know answers are not to be found here in Paris.'

'But the business ...'

'You would have to leave it.'

They went to bed not speaking to one another. Or, more correctly, with Jacques refusing to discuss the matter any further. But he could not sleep. Tossing and turning, he kept seeing brother Rombard's face looking at him. It glowed from the flames and gazed and gazed. It mattered little that Jacques shut his eyes, for even with his eyes shut he could see the eyes of brother Rombard weighing him.

At length, towards morning, he did fall asleep and he dreamt. This time it was his father-in-law's eyes that would not leave him. But his father-in-law's eyes were not filled with the knowledge that brother Rombard had. Rather they shone with a deadness that frightened Jacques. The pupils contained nothing, nothing at all. They looked out insensibly, holding no answers. And suddenly Jacques saw himself lying down in the street, in the same place that Maurice Caval had fallen. A black figure stood over him holding on to a rope. The rope was made of gold coins and tied around Jacques' neck.

Jacques' fingers groped about, trying to loosen the knot around his neck with one hand, yet, at the same time, not desiring to be loosened.

Suddenly a bright light such as he had never seen before, appeared. It was beyond him and he desired to be in that light, knowing it to be better than anything he had ever known. And then from out of the distant recesses of his mind he heard the words of brother Rombard echo down the street: 'Whatever takes a higher place in your life than the sovereignty of God, stands in the way of your salvation.' And the light faded and the coins constricted tight and tighter around his neck and he knew that he was dying.

But he did not die for when he opened his eyes he saw that he was lying in bed and that Aymee was already dressed and ready to go out.

'Where are you going?'

'To see some friends.'

She did not stop to speak and he was left alone in the bedroom. He cautiously raised his hand and moved his fingers. Dreams, he knew, were false and there was much work to be done today. Nevertheless the first thing he did was not to dress himself but to walk over to the wall, and count his money. Yet it did not give him the pleasure it had previously given him. Rather, he felt, in some strange measure, cheated. It was as if the coins had promised something and were now not living up to their end of the bargain.

'Are they higher?' he whispered, and then added another question, 'But is there a God?'

But he knew that there was a God. He knew it beyond a doubt. Perhaps he had repressed the knowledge; perhaps he had not desired it to be true; but he knew to within the marrow of his bones that God was real. And he felt His presence palpably as he looked at the stockpile of coins in front of him. But what was he to do? He tried to remember what brother Rombard had said.

'At every turn of your day, you must ... you must depend on God. In the beginning, the middle and at the end of the day you must totally depend upon Him.' Very well, Jacques thought, and in a surge of emotion he swept the coins off the bed. They flew to the floor, small and shiny, clattered for a moment and then lay mute and inanimate.

There was a knock at the door.

'Monsieur Dalierre! Monsieur Dalierre! Come quickly! There is a priest downstairs who wants to search the shop!'

Jacques put on his clothes as fast as he could and ran down the stairs to the workshop. There he found the priest from the procession in conversation with Aymee.

'You are of the new faith,' the man was saying and Aymee, his meek and reticent wife, nodded in assent.

'Yes, I am,' she said.

Jacques strode over.

'You have a reason for coming into my printing shop?'

'All printing shops, monsieur, are under scrutiny presently. Surely you know that. I have a special order from the bishop to search out and find those of the Huguenot persuasion. What about you, monsieur?'

'I want to ask you to leave these premises.'

'That does not answer the question, does it?'

The man stepped nearer and put his face close to that of Jacques.

'Between you and me, monsieur, you would do well to muzzle your wife. I am bound to take her in to the inquisitors, you know. And that would be a sad day for you, I am sure.'

A cold hand gripped Jacques' heart. Aymee stood quietly and smiled at him as if she had not a care in the world.

'You have credentials, sir?'

'My name is brother Parvant, monsieur, and, yes, I have credentials.'

He pulled out some documents and, after perusing them, Jacques nodded.

'Very well, I am sure you are a qualified churchman. However, I am equally sure that you, in all likelihood, are not overpaid. Is that not so, brother Parvant?'

'That is so, monsieur.'

'Perhaps then you would be so kind as to follow me up to my room, so that we can speak of the matter privately.'

Brother Parvant had no qualms about taking all the gold coins, every single one of them. Crawling about the bedroom like a baby, he picked up in haste, as if there were others who were in competition with him for the sum.

Jacques watched the undignified behaviour of the priest and felt strangely shed of manacles he had not known he wore. His skin tingled clean and healthy as a newborn. Aymee had followed them up and stood in the doorway, a serene look on her face.

The priest's cassock tinkled with the sound of the money and at length he was done. Standing up, his face shone red with exertion.

'I will give you three days to leave before I report to my superior.'

'Three days?' Jacques answered, 'Well, that is most kind, is it not, Aymee?'

Aymee stood aside to let the priest pass. His cassock touched her and she pulled away towards the wall. He felt her distaste and had the grace to look embarrassed.

They heard his footsteps shuffle down the rather steep stairs with some difficulty. Every now and then the clink of coins travelled up but the noise grew fainter and fainter. Aymee looked at her husband.

'Now,' she said, 'you are able to leave, I think.'

Jacques looked at the empty niche, at the clean floor and suddenly smiled.

'I have already left,' he answered.

*'For all the peoples walk each in the name of its god,
but we will walk in the name of the LORD our God
forever and ever.
In that day, declares the LORD,
I will assemble the lame and gather those who have
been driven away, and those whom I have afflicted;
and the lame I will make the remnant,
and those who were cast off, a strong nation;
and the LORD will reign over them in Mount Zion from
this time forth and for evermore.'*
(Micah 4:5-7)

Walk Only
With the Virtuous

There is this given – that either God exists or He does not. If a person fails to address this matter within himself, he is a fool and not concerned with matters of inevitable consequence. There may be times of eating and drinking; indeed, there may be times of great wealth. But always, even as a bird must at some time stop its soaring to alight somewhere, so a man must at some time dismount from life as from a horse. And where shall his foot land?

* * *

Between the pains Elizabeth thought herself in the chapel. There were angels carved on the end-posts of the stalls where she was wont to sit. They were seated, these angels, and had expressions of sweet mercy carved onto their wooden faces. As a child she had longed to touch these faces, but her mother had sharply reprimanded her whenever her body had leaned over, whenever her hand had dared to come close. Now, even as she breathed heavily, her hand reached back into her childhood and she imagined that she felt the smoothness of the wood. But when she touched the solid grain, the angels' faces remained impassively merciful, offering her no relief. It was a disappointment. She groaned. The midwife tutted as she stoked the coals in the stone fireplace and the fancy relief work of the chapel faded into lath and plaster ceiling beams.

'I pray to our Lady ...'

The words came as Elizabeth pushed.

'... help me ...'

The midwife was by her side now.

'... and all the saints ...'

Lewis Merton leaned against the wall in the hall to the right of the master bedroom. A chair had been brought for him but he paced about more than he sat. It seemed to him that birth was inexplicably tied up with death. He had stood godfather to a great many tenants' children and how many of those were living today? He could not at this present time recall. Elizabeth cried out and he walked over to the praying cross, a rectangular recess in the plaster of the wall next to the chair. Kneeling, he buried his face in his hands, saying between clenched teeth,

'Hail, Queen of heavens, hail, Mistress of the angels, hail, glorious Virgin, pray for us to Christ. Grant Elizabeth protection in her hour of need, so that she may rise in good health from this childbed, through the help of your intercession.'

He did not pray for the as yet unborn child. He already had a living child and heir and this second child's life did not overly concern him. Elizabeth's life did. He repeated the words of the prayer over and again like a child - he, Lewis Merton, who could trace his lineage back some three hundred years to the eleventh century.

There were families who needed to concoct ancestors for themselves, inventing an heroic past, but Lewis Merton had no need to do so. On top of his groats, half-groats, pounds, shillings, marks and silver coinage lay a document indicating that the Merton family had long had the privileges of nobility; that they had owned Ashridge Manor for many generations; that they had license to have a chaplain and conduct divine service; that they had tenants; that they executed wardship; and that they had married nobility.

A gentle cough behind Lewis caused him to stumble over his thoughts and falter in the words of his rote prayer.

'William would bid goodnight to his father.'

A small boy let go of his nurse's hand and walked up to Lewis. The round face was flushed and he appeared very grave.

'Shall I say prayers with you, sir?'

Lewis shook his head. It was quiet behind the bedroom door, ominously so, and he strained to hear.

'Sir?'

The boy knelt next to him and Lewis kissed the top of the fair head.

'You had best be off to bed, William.'

Signalling to the girl who had charge of him, he made as if to get up but the child stayed down and took hold of his father's sleeve.

'Sir, I would beg to tell you what Father Robb has told me.'

Father Robb was the manor priest. Lewis stayed where he was, partly because he was weary and partly because he loved William who was the replica of his mother. The child, encouraged by his father's silence, went on.

'Father Robb says that if you measure a body, head to foot, as you might measure for a coffin ...'

A coldness gripped Lewis. He sighed and put his head down again. The girl stepped forward to reach for William but perversely the child would not come, continuing rapidly.

'... and if you vow that person's length in silver, or maybe gold thread, to the Holy Mother, then that person will get better.'

Groans began to trickle out from under the door again and the girl forcibly pulled William up and away from his father.

'Come, young Master William, come. Your father must needs be alone now.'

The child went, although he looked over his shoulder a great many times before he reached the end of the hall.

A long hour later Elizabeth was delivered of a boy-child but Lewis had no eyes for the baby as he anxiously looked at his wife. She lay still, waxen white in appearance and the coldness, grown large in his belly, turned to ice. It was too late to measure her length with gold, or even with diamonds, for it would be to a coffin her body would go. It was the midwife who closed the dead mother's eyes for Lewis was caught up in devastation.

'The child lives, sir.'

The midwife laid the new-born down in the cradle next to Lewis as he knelt by the feather bed. She loosened the cloths that bound the baby so the father might properly inspect his limbs. The child kicked and began to wail as cool air touched his skin. Lewis turned his head and saw the child who was still covered with white vernix from the womb. He reached out and took hold of the boy's foot. The wailing stopped and eyes, round with newness and surprise, encompassed his own. The midwife stood close by. For a moment Lewis was overcome by the helplessness of the little one. He gently turned the boy onto his belly. The small legs pushed.

'There is a deformity, sir.'

Suddenly Lewis saw that the child had an unusual roundness in the spine, and he felt a great anger rising within him that Elizabeth should have died to give birth to a hunchback - a hunchback that lived. Turning his face away from the child, he pushed his hands into the feather bed, running them over the sheet as if he were wiping them.

'I shall name him Cain,' he said, 'for God has surely put a mark on this boy. Find him a wet nurse in one of the cottages.'

* * *

Ashridge Manor was situated in Kent. It was a good-sized manor, though perhaps not as large as others in Kent.

Nevertheless, it was self-sufficient and well-run, having some sixty tenants who all paid rent to Lewis Merton. He was a man of property, the size of which comprised more than eight hundred acres. The cottages milling together, not too far from the manor, had the makings of a small town. There were well-stocked stables, dove-houses, fodder-houses and kitchens. The land itself was arable, cleared of surrounding forest with but little swamp land.

Even as small Cain suckled at the bosom of one Margery Court, wife to one of the tenants, blissfully unaware of his father's dislike, his mother's body was carried from the manor house to Ashridge Chapel. Her cortege was headed by Father Robb. Six tenants, three on either side of the bier, carried torches. When the procession arrived at the chapel, it was greeted by several bell ringers. Dolorous and hollow the clappers rang and Elizabeth's body lay within the chapel for a full two days and nights before the funeral service was performed.

Margery Court carried the baby with her everywhere. Having lost her own infant just four days prior to Cain's birth, she felt some comfort in holding this deformed child, albeit not her own. She spoke to him as she cooked in the manor kitchen and she sang to him as she laundered manor clothes. More often than not Cain fell asleep to the sound of her voice as he swayed in the crook of her arm. Warm, fed and content he had no idea that his birth mother was being buried in the south aisle of Ashridge Chapel. Lewis had been careful to carry out the stipulations Elizabeth had made in her will. The aisle in the chapel was newly robed, leaded and glazed and a marble stone was commissioned - a stone which would bear the words, 'Here lies Elizabeth Merton, late the wife of Lewis Merton, daughter and heir of Ralph Hasting, April 7, 1518, on whose soul God have mercy.' The six tenants who had been chosen to hold torches at the burial were to be paid some money. Alms were to be distributed to all of the manor tenants and eight pounds of wax were to be given to Father

Robb so that candles could be lit daily before the image of the blessed Mary. As well, income from land that had belonged to Elizabeth was to go for a perpetual chantry, or mass, for her soul. A priest in Norwich was to be paid four pence a day to do this. All this Elizabeth had written out in her will, and all this Lewis had done, for he deemed this would guide her last footsteps to heaven.

If Cain thrived on Margery's milk, he also grew as he was dandled on Tom Court's knee. Tom and Margery had no surviving children of their own and the child, though deformed in body, had a friendly nature. He buried chubby fingers in Tom's beard and laughed in merriment when the burly farmer crawled about on all fours carrying the infant on his back. Tom would laugh too and Margery, though tired from her work at the manor and the drain on her body from feeding the child, was pleased to see her husband lavish care on a living baby. Sometimes she feared that Master Lewis Merton would come for the boy - would take him away to where they could no longer see him. But although occasional money was given to them through the bailiff, there was no message. When the boy turned three Tom even made so bold as to suggest to Margery that the child might follow him and be taught to hold the plough by the tail - be taught to till the land. Behind the small cottage, however, the shadows of gavelkind lurked, the old Kentish law which dictated that land was to be divided in equal shares between sons. Cain, deformed and unrecognised though he was, remained a Merton and brother to William. But Tom did not like to speak of these legal matters. He spoke only of what was in his heart.

'Who,' he asked Margery, as the next two years passed, 'is teaching the child to walk straight, to saddle a horse, to spit and turn, and to butcher?'

She did not answer.

'And what,' he went on, 'do others call the child if not Tom's Cain?'

Margery again did not answer. She felt there must be a good reason for the child's living with them. Life was not easy. Because there was not enough to feed the animals during winter, they were close to starvation by springtime. Swollen and bleeding gums prevailed in many homes. The filthy rotting of the walls of their small house caused ague and the sweating sickness. When Margery looked at the misshapen child, twice as susceptible with his hunchback load, she marvelled within herself that he was still living.

When Cain was almost six, Father Robb stopped by the cottage for a longer than usual visit. Conscientious and sober, he had shown increasing interest in the boy, suggesting from time to time that the lad might be good monk material.

'I have spoken to Master Merton,' he told Margery, 'and he agrees with me that the boy should know his letters.'

Father Robb himself had been educated at Eton, had gone on to Cambridge, and had the reputation of being an excellent scholar. Just three years prior to Cain's birth, he had been appointed to the surrounding district of Ashridge Manor, as well as having the charge of the manor chapelry itself. He was thirty-two years old, clear-eyed and the owner of a sizeable library.

'Come here to me, Cain.'

He spoke gently to the boy who readily walked over to him from where he had stood next to his surrogate mother.

'Would you like to learn how to read?'

The boy blinked rapidly, his great blue eyes diffused with wonder.

'To read?'

He repeated the words slowly.

'Yes, to read, Cain. You would come to my house and I would teach you your letters and you would learn to read.'

Cain looked up at Margery, who nodded briefly. Tom was not in the cottage.

'Would I still come home?'

Father Robb laughed.

'To be sure you would come home to Margery and Tom each evening and you could do them good cheer by reciting what you have learned, I think.'

Cain smiled.

'Then I will gladly come to your house, Father Robb.'

Father Robb's library consisted of forty-five large books covered with boards, forty smaller books also covered with board, and fifty books covered with leather and parchment. Cain was in awe. He had learned much from Tom, but more often than not, he was not able to lift or push or haul as the other children in the village could. But these books – now here was something he could lift. He held a piece of parchment in his hand and stroked the letters written upon it.

'Do you want to learn, Cain?'

The priest was amused by the child's behaviour.

'Oh, yes, Father.'

Cain could not explain to him the hunger within himself to hold knowledge – to grow in mind as indeed he knew by now, his body would not.

'Well, child, let us begin.'

Cain learned readily and unbeknownst to him, his progress was reported on a monthly basis to his father. Lewis Merton still had very little desire to see his misshapen hunchback child, but he did have a sense of lineage and this sense of lineage prevailed.

'I wish to know,' he told Father Robb, 'his disposition of wisdom. And although I do not wish him near me, I do wish him to be able to learn to become what he is meant to be ...'

Here his discourse stopped abruptly. Father Robb replied softly, astutely, wishing to heal the breach.

'Every poor man who has taken care of his children up to the age of twelve expects at that time to be helped and profited by them; likewise every highborn gentleman with discretion expects his kin, his kin that live by him and at his cost, to help him. As for your youngest son, he could greatly ...'

Master Merton interrupted.

'To be sure, Father, to be sure. Continue to teach him.'

And so Father Robb continued to teach.

'Make much of your father,' he told the child, 'and grieve him not as long as he lives.'

'What if he loves me not?'

'Master Merton, your father, loved your mother exceedingly. He misses her and when he sees you he is reminded of the fact that your birth brought him much sorrow.'

'My name, sir – why did my father call me Cain?'

'He was mistaken in his grief when he supposed that a crooked body meant a crooked heart. This, my boy, is not true and you must prove it to him.'

Father Robb was a true son of the Roman Catholic Church and as such, passed on the many false doctrines it embraced.

'It is important to hear mass, Cain. It is an enactment of the very sacrifice offered by Christ on Calvary to reconcile the human race with God; it is also a feast meant to feed the faithful on their journey to heaven.'

'Will I go to heaven, sir?'

'Perhaps, child, if you work hard.'

'How, sir?'

'Well, you must pray much to our Lady, hear mass on Sundays and Holy Days, abstain from eating meat on Fridays, and you must make sure to do good works.'

'What kind of good works? Are there any good works that might please my father, Master Merton?'

'Yes, Cain, there are.'

And so it was that the small boy spent several hours of each day in the chapel praying for his dead mother. Never mind that her body was buried underneath the south aisle and that prayers would not alter her eternal state. Father Robb's counsel was truth to the child and he steadfastly believed that these prayers would aid his mother's journey to heaven. He also believed that these prayers would, above all other things he did, please his father. Cain meant to please him, and Margery would shake her head at the child's knees, often raw from kneeling on the stone steps of the chapel. He was wont to say a prayer on each step, crawling to the next on all fours, scraping his flesh as he did so. Father Robb had told him that the drawing of blood brought merit both to himself and to his dead mother and that surely his mother was thankful to him on her way out of purgatory.

When Cain turned twelve he became aware that Father Robb's point of view was not the only point of view in the world. Itinerant preachers passed through the district from time to time. They dropped off pamphlets. The names Tyndale and Luther were bandied about. In the fall of 1530, a man spoke to Cain as he was praying his usual late afternoon shift of prayers in the chapel.

'Good afternoon, son.'

Cain turned his head, startled by the voice. Not many visited the chapel and he was used to being alone.

'Good afternoon, sir.'

The stranger, a tall man in a dark cloak, sat down on the chapel steps next to Cain.

'It is pleasant to see a young lad praying. I am sorry that I myself did not pray much when I was young.'

He smiled at Cain and Cain, in spite of his distrust of strangers who often made fun of his deformity, smiled back.

'My name is Richard Bridge. I am passing through these parts and am looking for a lodging place for the night.'

'I am sure my foster parents will be happy to give you lodgings, sir.'

Tom and Margery, always hospitable, had no qualms about opening their doors to Richard Bridge, who was a Protestant preacher. They were curious, as were many in England, what it was that made Protestants different and why Father Robb, and even the Pope, warned against them. A blustery wind blew about the cottage streets. A single candle guttered on the table and sparks flew off the logs Tom had put into the fireplace.

'Tell me, Master Bridge,' said Margery, uneasy as to what to call her visitor, who seemed equal to both Master Merton and Father Robb, but who all the same, she felt, would not be welcomed by them. 'Tell me. How is it that you follow Tyndale, the fellow Father Robb calls a savage Englishman?'

Cain sat watching the flames cast shadows on the man's face. He had a kindly face, the lad thought, and a ready smile.

'How is it I follow Tyndale?'

Richard Bridge repeated the question slowly and went on.

'Indeed, I do not follow Tyndale but the Word of God. Good wife, it is never people you must follow but only Jesus and what He teaches.'

'And so we do.'

Tom answered loudly, but not with certainty.

'We go to confession; we go to mass; and we show hospitality to the likes of folks such as yourself; and we ...'

Richard held up his hand.

'Fine good folk you appear to be, but where does the Bible tell you that you must go to confession and that a priest should mediate for you to God?'

It was quiet in the small cottage save for the crackling of the wood. Tom looked at Margery and she in turn looked at Cain. They could not read but the boy could quote a number of passages from the Bible. Cain swallowed.

'Father Robb says,' he began, lifting up his head so that it sank back against his hump, '... he says that confession is one of the seven sacraments. Sins must be repented and confessed to a priest before they take hold of your soul. Then these sins must be paid for by what the priest tells you to do.'

Richard Bridge smiled at Cain.

'You have learned your lessons well, lad. And so I once thought too. But when I began to read and study the Bible for myself, instead of just listening to what others told me, I noted that our blessed Saviour did not ordain confession. No, indeed, confession to a priest was something invented by man.'

Margery and Tom watched and so did Cain as their visitor took a book out of his cloak and opened it.

'The Word of God,' he said softly, gently turning pages, 'fresh off the press and translated at the risk of his life by the savage Englishman himself – Tyndale.'

Cain stared at the book. Father Robb only let him read certain passages. He had never held an entire Bible.

'Listen carefully,' Richard continued, 'for these words were written by John, beloved apostle of our Lord Jesus. John says, 'If we confess our sins, He (that is God) is faithful and righteous to forgive us our sins and to cleanse us from all unrighteousness.''

He closed the Bible again.

'Do you note that no priest is mentioned in these words? These words do away with confession booths - with the power of penance given by all priests such as your Father Robb. Do you see that every believing man is himself a priest and that you need no black-robed man to mediate between you and God at all?'

They saw Richard Bridge off and on through the next years. He travelled up and down the countryside as did many others like him. King Henry VIII's lustful desire for divorce from his Catholic bride had given Protestants a certain measure of freedom. And although King Henry may have thought he was in charge of the church, providence is a strange, fearful and all-encompassing thing. For the truth of the matter was that God caused good to come out of the human passions Henry entertained. Many changes were born into the English church. Clerical marriages became acceptable to some monks and a number of them left their monasteries to preach true and free salvation. There were other monks, however, who became deeper entrenched in man-made rules, scourging themselves in the privacy of their cells until their stammels, their coarse woollen robes, were red with blood.

Cain listened closely to Richard Bridge when he passed through the area. He liked the man whose knowledge seemed to surpass that of Father Robb. And Richard Bridge loved the wide-eyed, solitary child.

'Elijah and Elisha were not the first monks, Cain. Father Robb is wrong. There is no reason given in the Bible for monasteries, boy.'

'Father Robb and ... and my own father, Master Lewis Merton at the manor ... they say I should become a monk ...

that because of ... because of my ... my deformity ... it is meet that I should ... that God desires of me to live in a monastery.'

Cain spoke falteringly.

'Is this what you want, Cain? Is this what you would do?'

The fourteen-year-old boy shook his head - his head which ever seemed too small for the body beneath it.

'Well, then you need not become a monk, Cain.'

'But if Master Merton, my father, if he has taken a hand in the matter, great harm is likely to come of it if I refuse. It would be considered a disworship to him considering that I ... that I am his son and known as such.'

Although Cain was accepted in and around the manor, people never quite understood his place. He worked the fields from time to time with Tom, spitting and turning, hedging and ditching, but he also studied with Father Robb. Besides this he came and went freely to and from the manor house. No one ever saw him in conversation with either his father or his brother William, yet all knew he was a son as well as William was a son and that the estate would be divided equally between the two. No bedroom was assigned to Cain at the manor but when he chose to sleep there, a matter which no one ever prevented, he went up to the servants' quarters in the attic. He felt as at home there as he did in Tom's cottage. It was a vast place, running the length of the house. Thick planks provided flooring and the area was broken up into two sections. The unmarried male servants slept over the master bedroom and the unmarried female servants had their truckle beds or straw mattresses on the other side of the attic. A partition of cow-dung plaster separated the two sides.

When Cain was a child of eleven he had discovered a loose board in the attic floor, which, when he lifted it, exposed his father's study. Every now and then the boy would lie on his stomach, carefully lift the plank and study Lewis as he sat down at his desk. He did not blame the man for not wanting him, for was he not different than all the other boys he knew. His father's statement that God had surely put a mark on him was an added weight on his hunched shoulders.

He had prayed many times on his knees, even as he had prayed for his dead mother, that the blessed Lady might take away the shame of the hump but surely his prayers were tainted.

He had also vowed to go on a pilgrimage when he was older, perhaps to Canterbury, or perhaps to the throne of Saint Peter in Rome. And whenever Margery received money from the steward for her keep of him, he begged for a quarter penny. The odd times she gave in, he had walked to the chapel and had put it into the alms box. As it dropped with a clink, he would drop to his knees and pray that the disgrace of his disfigured body might be taken away. Father Robb commended him for his self-degradation and said that his mother surely would have been proud of him for this. Above the words of his mother Elizabeth's grave was carved the figure of a gentlewoman in her mantle. Cain often stood by the stone, thinking how it would have been had she lived and had he not had such a hump on his back.

One afternoon as Cain lay on his belly in the attic watching his father sit at some paperwork, his brother William came in. William was twenty-one and a tall, sturdy young man. He came to speak of marriage and Cain heard only snatches from his perch above their heads.

'... eighteen ... an only child ... She will bring property with revenue ... Looks healthy ... Her father appeared quite willing ... Will inherit land from Stanstead in Suffolk after his death ... If it goes through, what land shall we give to her as dower?'

The marriage plans were no surprise to Cain. The servants had talked and he had two good ears.

'... and what of Cain, sir.'

Upon hearing his own name, the boy became tense. He rarely, if ever, heard his name mentioned by either William or his father.

'Well, what of him?'

'Is he to inherit with me, sir?'

William stood facing his father.

'You have always said that he would die before he was ten with that cursed weight on his shoulders and look ...'

Cain gripped the loose plank and the hump burned on his back. He saw his father turn and walk directly underneath him.

'The boy will not inherit.'

'You have suffered him this long ...'

William walked towards where his father stood and continued his words.

'... and I have often heard it said that the hump was the devil's mark on him. Indeed ...'

Lewis did not move and Cain's breath came unsteadily as if someone held his heart in a vice grip. He only half heard his father's reply.

'I have sent a trusty man to Covethite ... there are unemployed sailors there who will hire out as ...'

Cain did not catch the next part. The beating of his heart was so loud it drowned out all other noise. But he understood this - that both his father and his brother meant him harm.

* * *

'Master Merton means to mischief you!'

Cain had haltingly relayed to Margery what he had heard and she immediately began to urge the boy to travel to London, to seek out a position.

'In good faith, no creature can imagine how foul and horrible an end you will come to if you do not leave here. I think it is William's doing - I think he is pushing your father ... I have seen William strike Geoffrey Allan for not having his rent on time and often William is drunk. You dare not go about here any longer, Cain, for who would protect you if he, and some cut-throats he has hired, tried to waylay you one dark evening, and you but a lad and not strong at that.'

Cain looked at Tom who sat silently by the hearth. Here was a sweeter father than Lewis Merton had ever been. When Tom said nothing Cain moved closer to the flames and perceived that the man was weeping into his big fists. He spoke softly.

'I pray you, Tom, do not take it too hard, for I know well I am near your heart ...'

Then Tom lifted his head and bellowed out his grief.

'I shall defend you boy! I shall fight anyone ...'

'Hush now.'

Margery was quick to come to his side.

'It is better to not voice threats, husband, nor that you should implicate others who would help you protect the lad. Leave these things to God, even as good Master Bridge taught us we should not offend conscience. And you know full well that if the boy be gone for a while, Master Merton may surely repent of his evil intent and I shall pray God it might be soon. I beg you, Tom, for my heart's ease, be of good comfort in this and do nothing rash.'

'You would suffer Cain to be in jeopardy with no help. You would ...'

Tom almost choked on his indignation as Margery's hand closed over his mouth.

'Hush, husband, and listen.'

She slowly took her hand away from his mouth.

'It is clear that Cain must leave. So I say he should go to London. That city is so large no one will ever find him. Why, if there were a hundred hired to harm the boy, that city is so vast ...'

'It is too vast. He will die losing his way either before he gets there or once he arrives there. There are twisted lanes and dark alleys, I have heard tell, at every turn ... pick-pockets, cut-throats ...'

'No, Tom. He won't lose his way. He can travel on with Master Bridge when next he passes through ... although I think that is not soon enough. I trow he could also ride to London in the trade cart with Peter Wykes who is due at the manor day after tomorrow. I dare say I could make a bargain with Wykes to have Cain tucked away in his wagon.'

Cain and Tom were both quiet for a moment and then Tom spoke again, his voice becoming louder at every sentence.

'And pray, even if there were means to bring Cain to London, what shall the lad do once he is there? Who will be friendly or neighbourly to him? He shall have less help or comfort in that place than he does here where there are those who love him.'

'Master Bridge spoke to me of Cain last time he was here. He said that should the lad wish to do something else instead of tarrying here waiting to see if he be sent to a monastery ... well, then he should have that right. Master Bridge gave me a letter addressed to someone he knows at Blackfriars in London.'

'Who?'

'A German merchant, a Master Lander, who may have need of someone to do some work for him.'

The upshot of the matter was that at two the next morning Cain was wakened by Margery, provisioned with a bag of bread, and bid Godspeed.

'Peter Wykes will watch for you tomorrow by the second finger-post to London. Keep to the left of the road, lad. Sleep in a hawthorn hedge this night. Avoid all people even if you know them and ...'

Margery stopped. She wiped her eyes and then held open her arms to the only son she had ever known. Fleetingly Cain thought of the grave in the south-aisle of Ashridge Chapel. The white, cold marble on which he had bruised his knees contrasted sharply with the soft bosom which now enfolded him. And later on, as he trudged along the ill-kept highroad, the memory of her warmth was a comfort to him.

The sun rose and the birds sang - the throstle, the lark and the golden-billed ouzel – all selling to Cain the beauty of the countryside and the sweetness of an open, rosy sky. At six he sat down on a tract of brushwood and ate some bread. Cattle grazed nearby on a common waste of heath and a flock of geese nipped grass. He did not rest long, but got up again shortly, stretching his tired limbs before he did so. The road was in poor condition, dusty and filled with pot-holes. Yet on either side the buttercups glowed and Cain had an urge to sing - and so he did.

'O the month of May, the merry month of May!
So frolic, so gay, and so green, so green, so green!'

At noon he drank by the side of a stream and then slept a while, waking refreshed. It was a long afternoon and he met but a few people on the road and all strangers. He bore Margery's advice in mind and kept to himself. Winding lanes diverged off the main road from time to time and often he was tempted to turn into a pleasant looking bit of road. Occasionally a flock of sheep crossed his path and in the evening lazy columns of smoke coiled up from cottages nearby. The sight of the smoke brought the first pangs of homesickness to Cain for he longed for the hearth and board he had known since childhood. He propped himself up by a log eating more of the bread Margery had wrapped in a cloth. The crust fed him a taste of home and this was where he now longed to be. Standing up slowly after his supper, he decided to find a comfortable spot to bed down while it was still light enough to see. Shortly afterwards he found a pretty lane, meandering like a stream through a wooded area. After walking down it a while, Cain became increasingly uneasy. Dusk was rapidly falling, trees cast whimsical shadows and the sound of his footsteps seemed abnormally loud. He also fancied hearing faint rustles and voice-like sounds behind him. Pursing his lips for a whistle, no song would leave his mouth. He tried to recall how he had felt earlier on in the day, when the sun had warmed him and when the hours had seemed full of promise. There was no comfort in the hour that now surrounded him – no comfort at all.

What was comfort? The wind rustled overhead and Cain was somehow reminded of Master Bridge's earnest teaching.

'There is comfort in this world and the next, lad - very sure comfort. I recommend it to you heartily – to hang about your neck daily as an easement for your spirit.'

'What is this comfort?'

Margery had leaned forward as she sat by the table. Cain could see her now, eyes half-shut in concentration as she peered at Master Bridge across from her.

'That you, Margery Court, and you, Tom Court, and you, Cain Merton ... that all three of you belong, body and soul, in life and in death, not to yourselves but to Jesus ...'

Richard Bridge had stopped and had looked at each of them intently.

'And, my good friends, weep for joy, for this Jesus, with His blood, has paid for all your sins – all of them. And He has also delivered you from the power of the devil. Do you understand?'

They had, all three of them nodded – nodded solemnly.

'Well then, that is comfort. No more penance or confessions! There is nothing to fear from hell-fire!'

An early owl hooted and brought Cain out of his reverie - almost but not quite - for he went on to remember Richard Bridge's parting line as he had left that evening. He repeated the words out loud.

'Your Father in heaven cares deeply for you, lad. Not a hair can fall from your head, Cain, without your Father's will. Not a hair, my lad, not a hair.'

Now as the darkness deepened, Cain reached up and touched his hair, even as his foot shot out and kicked a rock on the pathway. It was not really a path anymore, merely a sheep track. He was suddenly weary, bone-weary with the long day and sat down in the undergrowth, resting his rounded back against a tree stump. The tremulous strain of a nightingale began somewhere overhead. He was not afraid any more for it seemed to him in a strange manner, that he was not alone. Indeed, he felt fellowship to be so tangible that he could almost touch it. But there was no one around, so perhaps it was only the memory of Tom, Margery and Master Richard Bridge. Folding his hands, he prayed and, after the prayer, curled up on his side and slept.

At noon the next day, even as Margery had envisioned, Peter Wykes rode up in his trade cart behind the lad and took him on to London.

* * *

From the very first glimpse he had of it, Cain disliked the city of London. The rather broad road they had come on, although rife with holes, was soon transformed into a much narrower street. Wykes, upon entering the city, had almost immediately turned down one of the many rubble and mud alleys of London. Houses on either side of the cart rose three or four storeys. Their overhanging levels encroached upon the sky and obliterated light. The walls of the uneven structures seemed to Cain to be tilting towards him and he felt choked, deprived of air. There were more people about than he had ever seen in his entire life. The hustling and hurried commotion around the hundreds of roadside stalls was deafening. The noise of thousands of people bargaining, gesturing, and jostling to get about, frightened him and he was glad Wykes slowly but surely manoeuvred the cart along. Squalor, stench and commotion effectively numbed him to where he was going or why he was actually in London.

It was late afternoon when Wykes stopped in front of a rather large house. Located in a poor stretch of street, it was not a house of note, and actually made a poor impression on Cain. The roof was slate and the wood and plaster beneath it desperately sagged.

'Your Master Lander's house.'

Peter Wykes made no effort to dismount and to Cain's dismay, the man drove off as soon as the lad jumped down from the cart. The swaying sign above a nearby door advertised a tavern and he heard raucous laughter. He cautiously approached the door of the house Wykes had indicated and knocked. A passing street-boy shoved him in the back and he was knocked down onto the ground.

'Hey, hunch-back, what ails you? Cannot you carry your own weight?'

The door opened and a kindly looking man peered down at him. Cain got to his feet and looked up uncertainly.

'Well, junglein, you must be the young mann Richard Bridge has sprechen me about. Komm in, freund, komm in. Ich habe kein use for the night air und du bist mude, tired. Komm, fur a draught of ale. Thirsty weather, travelling. Komm in, junglein, komm in.'

And Cain came in.

Master Johann Lander, a German merchant of the Steelyard, had resided in London for a number of years. A confirmed bachelor, he employed a capable housekeeper who saw to his needs. He was also moderately wealthy and Cain was amazed to find that the dingy looking house contained a fine interior. Behind the squalid street entrance lay a number of fine rooms as well as a broad garden. Every morning, Master Lander walked to Blackfriars, to an enclave called the Stalgard, or Steelyard, a courtyard for the display of sample goods. All the merchants here were members of the Hanseatic League and, as such, were exempt from English jurisdiction. They governed by their own alderman and Council of Twelve who administered German law.

Lander was an astute and very honest merchant. He employed several buyers and two apprentices who worked for him at the Steelyard and who also had rooms there. Cain expected that he would be put to work there as well and was agreeably surprised the very first morning when, after having breakfasted together on a little bread and butter washed down with a pot of ale, Master Lander pushed his chair away from the table and regarded the boy somewhat solemnly.

'Well, Cain, willt du lehren?'

'Lehren?'

'Ja, lehren - to learn - do you want to learn?'

'Yes, I do.'

Johann Lander smiled.

'Das ist gut.'

Cain was nonplussed.

'Zwei things I would have you to do. Zwei ...'

'Zwei?'

Lander held up two fingers, and Cain understood.

'Oh, two.'

'Ja, two things. First is du musst Frau Green helfen.'

Cain nodded. He understood that he was to help the housekeeper.

'Gut. Und du must in Mittag komm hier und ich will mit ...'

Cain looked increasingly puzzled and his host stopped. He stood up and walked over to a bookcase. Taking out two books, he brought them over to the boy. One was a Latin primer and the other was a Bible - an English Bible.

'We're going to read together?'

Lander smiled broadly.

'Ja, read together. Wir lehren together.'

In a surprisingly short time, Cain had settled into a routine. Each morning, after an early breakfast with Johann Lander, he helped the housekeeper, Abigail Green, to shop for food. Stalls clustered about everywhere in the narrow streets. After a few days, he began to know his way about, and could read the signs swinging from the various shops with understanding - a bush indicated the vintner, three gilded pills meant the apothecary, a white arm with red stripes told him a barber-surgeon resided there, a unicorn meant a goldsmith and a horse's head a harness maker. Every morning Cain, carrying a large basket, walked behind the housekeeper who pinched fowl, squabbled over prices and tasted ale to see if it was watered down. Peddlars' cries selling fish, garlic, honey, onions, fruit, eggs, and leeks filled his ears and he only thought of Ashridge Manor every now and then - only missing Margery and Tom when he crawled into bed at night.

After a good walk with Abigail, which could take a few hours, Cain was delegated to other tasks. She taught him how to cook. As well, under her supervision, he shook out cushions and covers; he emptied the chamber pots; he made up the kitchen fire; he filled the water vat and the big iron kettle in the kitchen and he swept out the entrance and the hall. He also weeded the small herb garden Abigail had cultured and this he liked most of all the chores she assigned to him.

A year went by. Sometimes the thought of his past life, of his real father, overwhelmed Cain. This was mostly after visits by Richard Bridge. Every few months the itinerant preacher stopped by to see his friend Johann Lander and the two men, having sent Cain to bed by midnight, would talk well into the small hours of the morning. Cain would listen to the city watch under his window,

Give ear to the clock,

beware your lock,

your fire and your light,

and God give you good night --

One o'clock.

He would smile under his dagswain blanket and feel comforted that these two men, whom he could still hear passionately speaking of their love for God, cared about him also and how strange it was that he loved them so even though they were not kin. Richard Bridge told him about Margery and Tom, of how they were hale and sent him many greetings, and how they prayed God would keep him in good health. Cain never asked about Lewis Merton, his father. Indeed, it seemed to him that his tongue cleaved to the roof of his mouth if he so much as thought about speaking a word of the man. He was becoming more and more familiar with what the Bible taught and Johann, as well as Richard Bridge when he was visiting, was patient with him, explaining at length doctrines Cain had never before known.

A year and a half after his arrival in London, Richard Bridge arrived one evening carrying a packet for Cain. It was from Father Robb, he said, for Cain. Cain received the packet somewhat awkwardly and took it up to his room. Unwrapping it as he sat on the edge of his mattress, he felt strange, as if he were unravelling a piece of comfortable shirt which he had worn a long time and which he had no desire to unravel. A ring fell out of the packet, his father's ring. It rolled onto the floor and circled, circled, until it at last fell down. A small black ribbon was attached to the ring. He looked at the ring for a long time without picking it up. It was a large ring, a signet ring and even though it was dark in the room, he could see its glitter. He had often seen that glitter as he had watched his father from his perch in the attic. A coldness gripped him and he remembered – remembered how his father and his brother William had purposed to harm him.

Later that night, Richard Bridge came up to Cain's room. Cain was not asleep and silently looked at the man as he stood in the door opening.

'May I come in?'

Cain nodded.

'Have you opened the packet yet?'

Cain nodded again.

'Father Robb asked me to tell you that your brother William died.'

Cain lay very quietly. His eyes were riveted onto Bridge's face. He said nothing.

'William had an accident. I do not know what happened.'

Cain still did not respond.

'I do know that now is the time for you to return home. Indeed, Cain, I counsel you to do so. Perhaps the ill-will your father has born you so long has abated and he would fain ask your forgiveness. You must try and hear him make amends.'

Cain pulled the blanket over his head and sought to block out Richard Bridge's words. He was happy here. To be sure, it was not his real home. He was dependent on the gratuitous hospitality of Johann Lander, but surely at some point he would be able to repay the man.

'Cain! Cain, listen to me. I can travel with you most of the way. I do not have the leisure to travel as far as Ashridge Manor, but I can accompany you a good length. Son, Almighty God has you in His keeping and will provide you with His care. Has He not always done so? Now you must trust and do what is proper.'

'Auf wiedersehen.'

It was all the farewell Johann Lander gave the boy the next morning and later, walking on the road, Cain asked Richard Bridge what the words meant.

'The words mean,' till we see one another again.'

'How does he know that we will?'

Cain's words were bitter for he truly had no desire to leave the London house behind him. It had been a surety in a time when he had been afraid. Johann had become a second surrogate father and Abigail Green had taken the place of Margery.

'He knows that you will see one another again because you are both believers in Christ Jesus. Believers need never say goodbye because they will always see one another again.'

The din of the congested London streets throbbed about them. Once they passed over the bridge and turned onto Watling Street, however, things became quieter. It was a broad street which, though filled with holes and ruts, was cemented here and there with brushwood. A few miles out of London its broadness dwindled somewhat and Cain and Richard had to straddle their way past bushes which had overgrown onto the road. Every now and then a cart lumbered by.

'How have you been since I last saw you, Cain?'

Cain shrugged. Still unhappy about leaving Lander's home, he was not in the mood for talking. Richard Bridge was not deterred.

'I told you that Margery sends you God's blessing and her love. She would have you at home with her. And she said also that once you have met again, you shall not lightly leave until death parts you.'

'Margery was the one who sent me to London. I was undone at the time. But she would have me go ...'

'She thought it dangerous for you to be at the manor at the time, Cain, even as she also believes it is safe for you to return now. Do not take her care for you to displeasure. Can you not see that it was plain to her at the time that you should go.'

Cain smiled at last, his head tilted back against his hump.

'I know. I can say no more but sapienti pauca, as Master Lander always says. 'A word to the wise is sufficient'. But I am only a hunchback and not so wise.'

'Does it bother you greatly, Cain. Your hump, I mean?'

Richard had never before spoken of Cain's deformity. Cain was quiet for a long while and his companion was afraid he had offended him. But at length he replied.

'It bothered me not when I was little. For I was loved and coddled by Margery and Tom. Indeed they loved me as if they were my own parents. And when one is loved I think one always feels beautiful, or handsome, if you will.'

He was quiet again for a spell and then continued.

'It is when you sense that others do not care for you; it is when you notice that people are not at ease with you; it is then that you become bothered. It is so fortuned that my stature is grotesque. The very sight of me makes others uneasy.'

'You know, do you not, Cain, that God looks at a man's heart and not at his outward appearance.'

'There is somewhat that troubles me, Richard. For in Genesis I read with Master Lander that God has made us in His likeness. Well then, is He a hunchback like myself – or is he straight-shouldered like you?'

Richard was silent and the lad went on.

'I know that I am like others in that I eat, speak, weep and laugh as they do. And yet, and yet I am not the same. For I see no others bearing this burden, this weight of stone, this mark, as my father said when I was born.'

Richard reached out to touch the lad, but Cain shrank from his touch and moved to the side of the path.

'Often, Cain, God gives us something, something difficult, to draw us closer to Him. For some it is one thing and for others something else.'

'Indeed.'

Cain spoke coldly, almost as if he regretted making himself more vulnerable than he already was. He continued.

'Indeed. Pray tell what God has given you to draw you closer to Him?'

'I saw my mother and father and six brothers and sisters die of the plague. And all in the space of two days.'

Richard fell silent now and they walked on. The morning was fair and bright. The song of small birds twittered about them and a deer suddenly broke their path by jumping gracefully out of the bushes and running on into the undergrowth on the other side.

'How long before you must turn off?'

Suddenly troubled by the fact that Richard Bridge would leave him at some point and that he must carry on the journey alone, Cain eyed his travelling companion anxiously.

'Not until sometime tomorrow. And then you shall not be far from Ashridge Manor.'

Actually when the time came to part company, Cain was not as fearful as he had thought he would be. There were but a few hours of travel ahead of him and Richard had assured him time and again that his father would very likely be glad to see him.

'This day seven nights from now, I trust I shall visit you at Ashridge Manor. And I also trust I shall find you hale and hearty and I do not intend to depart until I have spoken with you about all that shall have passed and all that lies in the future. For truthfully, Cain, you will inherit property and many people shall have help and comfort from you. This is God's design.'

'Perhaps. As for my coming home, I know no certainty and will not until I see Master Merton, my ... my father.'

'I trust God will see to you in all matters right well, lad.'

It was dusk when Cain began to recognize familiar landmarks. He did not make straight for the manor but instead headed for the chapel. It was strange now to think of the many hours he had spent here in prayer, of the countless petitions he had offered up on the grave of his mother. 'Here lies Elizabeth Merton, late the wife of Lewis Merton, daughter and heir of Ralph Hasting, 7th April, 1518.' He traced the cold letters with his fingers. And where was she now, this mother of his? He shivered. A light patter on the roof told him that it had begun to rain. And yet he lingered. Shadows deepened. Within himself he knew that he did not want to see anyone yet, or more truthfully, he wanted no one to see him.

When the sun had set completely, Cain made his way to the manor. He knew the way well enough for how often had he not felt his way through total darkness to this place? How often had he not peeped through the shuttered window to watch his father lounge about, even as he had silently watched him past the loose board in the attic? On an impulse he swung from the stone path onto the lawn and slowly walked towards the study window. The silence was tangible and his footsteps, though muffled by the grass, seemed uncommonly loud. He reached the shutters and found that the rock he had been wont to stand on so long ago, was still in place. Stepping onto it, he craned his neck and tilted his head. He could see his father sitting at his desk. Several candles burned, papers cluttered about and a fire burned in the hearth. He stared a good five minutes before the position cramped his shoulders. His father had not shifted or moved even once in all that time. He seemed to be holding a scroll. Cain moved to change his footing and slipped. Falling backwards into the bushes, he made enough noise to cause those inside to be alarmed. He lay motionless for a few moments, but when he heard nothing he got up again and resumed his stand on the rock. His father still sat at the desk, seemingly staring at the scroll. The scene made Cain slightly uncomfortable. Something was not quite natural. Swinging open the shutters, he was able to pull himself over the window ledge, landing awkwardly on the window seat.

His father's face did not turn nor did he move to greet Cain. The boy boldly stepped past the two suits of armour which flanked the east window and came nearer the desk. Physically he had never been in the study before. Ranged along elaborate wainscotting and various tapestries, a map of England, Scotland and Ireland was framed in dark oak. He slowly moved past the chart. The thick layers of rushes on the floor gave off a sweetish odour of new-mown hay.

'Father?'

Cain's voice was uncertain. A calculating board lay on the desk, as well as a pair of scales, scissors, a foot ruler, seals, a quill and a large pewter inkstand.

'Father?'

Cain repeated the word, moving closer and closer. With dismay he noted the glazed look in his father's eyes. Near enough now to touch, he leaned over and felt the hand holding the scroll. The candles flickered at the motion. The hand was almost, but not quite, cold. A shudder ran through the boy.

'Father?'

He repeated the word for the third time but he was never to have an answer for he knew with a surety that his father was out of his time, was beyond his call, and was unable to answer. He pulled his arm back with a jerk and the scroll of paper fell off the desk onto the dead man's lap. It had writing on it, lately written, still moist with ink. Walking around the desk Cain gingerly picked it up. His father's breeches were made of satin. He noted it at the same time as he noted that the document was addressed to himself.

'To my son and heir, Cain Merton.'

The phrase blazed out at him and he carefully carried the scroll over to the hearth. Taking some ashes, he spread these over the page to dry the small, spider-like scrawl of his father's words. Then he sat down to read.

To my son and heir, Cain Merton.

There are diverse things I would have you know before I die. Tom and Margery Court do both tell me that you should verily be home ere long. But I do not know if I shall live to see you. Indeed, I am fairly certain that it is not well with me.

It is right long since I have had tidings from you and please you to understand that I would beg your forgiveness for such things as have passed. It does burden me right heavy that I may not tarry long in this world and beseech you, if you read these words, that you may consider my past mischief against you as having come from one who did consider bad advice as better than sound advice. I do repent it and rue the day you left. But I shall not burden you with the uneasiness of my soul but shall relate to you what has happened to your brother William before I am unable to do so. It is meet that you should know about your brother, for you may learn, indeed I pray you shall, from his life.

William was a sweet child and indeed, the apple of his mother's eye while she lived. And when she died, I doted on him, for I wrongly perceived that by giving him things, I was giving them to my sweet Elizabeth, your mother. And I fear this was his undoing.

Although he did well, he learned from me no disposition of wisdom, nor did he grow in self-control such as an heir to Ashridge Manor ought to have. It is the truth that even though William was strong and able of mind, he never, when he grew older, stood me in profit nor did he ever help any one if the deed did not profit himself. An ill thing to say of one's own son. But so it was and now, with the clarity of hindsight, I do see how the poor upbringing I provided caused no weal.

As it is he holds no title to the manor. For he is dead. Did you know? He was thrown from his horse and brought home a fortnight ago, lifeless and not mourned by any save me. There was little love lost betwixt him and the people of the manor. He was often cruel and unjust as he went about with the bailiff collecting rents. My shame is that I knew but did nothing. And my penance is loneliness and grief.

The story the tenants tell in jest of William's death grieves me and even though I know it is but a legend, an old wives' tale, it frightens me to think they use it on my kin. And so I pass it on to you in sorrow. Listen and read, my son ...

Cain stopped reading for a moment and looked at the bright flames in the hearth. Never in all his born days had his father spoken to him and to be spoken to now and in such a manner unsettled him. He was unsure of all the feelings springing up within himself. Inadvertently he looked up at the great ceiling above his head. The heavy timbers, rich with design, sheltered the attic and held the place he had often sat in looking out at his father while he worked at his desk. Slowly he lowered his gaze and continued his father's small chronicle.

... This is what they say happened to William. They say that while he rode to collect the rents, he met the devil who asked him where he was going.

William replied that he was on his way to collect rent. The devil then asked him if he would take whatever was freely offered to him.

William answered that he would and in turn asked the devil where he was going.

The devil replied that he was also collecting but that he would not take whatever men gave, but only whatever men gladly gave, with their whole heart and soul.

The two travelled some distance together and saw a ploughman commending his oxen, who had stubbornly strayed from their course, to the devil.

'These oxen are obviously yours,' William said, but the devil shook his head.

'I think not,' he replied, 'for the farmer gives not from the heart.'

A little while later they passed a cottage and heard a disobedient child mocking and his mother wishing him to the devil.

'The child is yours,' William said again. 'I think not,' the devil replied 'for in her soul she does not really want to lose her son.'

At length the pair came to a very poor cottage, whose poverty-stricken widow had only one cow which had been taken by William the previous day. When the widow saw William, she screamed at him, 'To all the devils of hell I commend you!'

At this moment the devil took hold of William and exclaimed, 'Well, there is no doubt that you, in any case, are mine.' And he bore him away to hell.'

Cain glanced at the dead figure of his father by the desk. And he shivered in spite of the nearness of the flames of the hearth. Had he ever envied William? Had he ever desired to lead his brother's life? The scroll slipped from his hands and he noted that they bled cold sweat. Picking the paper up again, he turned back to the words his father had written.

'... It was well that you did leave this place. I do not know how it was conveyed to you, but in truth, I did for a few foul days wish you harm.

And so, I write this in shame and full repentance thereof, I hired men to waylay you, to harm you and indeed, to murder you. Ah, this small scroll is a confession booth. Do you mind how Father Robb would hear confession? 'Have you spent Sunday in shooting, wrestling, and other play? Have you found anything and kept it? Have you borrowed anything and not returned it? Have you ever claimed a deed of charity that was another man's doing? Have you missed mass? Have you been glad when a friend came to harm or grieved when a neighbour had good fortune? Have you eaten like a glutton? Have you given alms grudgingly?'

Before God I say that any of these and all of these are nothing compared to the sin of harbouring murder in my heart – and murder of my own child. It has eaten me up this past year and more.

'But, praise God, the truth is that no foul deed was done. The men I hired came back to me and relayed that they had been unable to come near you. They did track you as you walked away from Ashridge Manor and upon the evening of that same day you left they say that you turned off the main road onto a small path. They lauded their good fortune for they thought that there, on a side road, they would indeed be free to go about their evil business. With their daggers drawn they were close enough to you, they told me, to note that you spoke to yourself. But suddenly, and they said they knew not how or when this happened, there was a company of men about you. And these men, they said, were clothed in light and shining coats, a matter very apparent to them as it was rapidly growing dark. These men were a hedge about you and put the fear of God into the hearts of the murderers I had hired. They told me all this in great agitation, returning the money I had given them in mortal anxiety for their souls.*

'When you were born I named you Cain, saying God had put His mark on you. Well, so He did ...'

The writing ended suddenly, and Cain let the scroll drop from his hands. Then he rose and walked over to his father. Gently closing the eyelids, he leaned the body back in the chair, speaking softly as he did so.

'May God have mercy on your soul.'

* * *

There is this given - that either God exists or He does not. And the truth is that the matter will be addressed by all at death. There may be times of sweetness and laughter; indeed, there may be times of overflowing abundance. But always, even as the oak must drop its leaves to stand naked, so a man must shed his life as a well-worn coat. And what shall he then be given to clothe himself with? What indeed?

'For if the blood of goats and bulls,
and the sprinkling of defiled persons with the ashes of a
heifer, sanctify for the purification of the flesh,
how much more will the blood of Christ,
who through the eternal Spirit offered himself without
blemish to God, purify our conscience from dead works
to serve the living God.'
(Hebrews 9:13-14)

FROM DEAD WORKS

A girl, wrapped from head to feet in a brown, woollen robe, and carrying a staff, spoke crossly as a party of four trudged wearily across country roads. 'If only you had not made so free with the wine, this morning ...'

The stretches of path actually hardly deserved the name as there were great lengths filled with ruts, boulders and knee-high grass. No one deigned to respond to the girl. They walked in single file as the path was thin and unfriendly, not given to any pairing of travellers. Two men carrying packs were at the front; the girl and an older woman made up the tail.

'Overloading the donkey and then not holding onto the rope properly. How anyone could be so doltish, I'm sure I don't know!'

The sky, as well as the statement, was heavy with storm. In spite of that, a lark sang overhead, sweet and pure, crickets chirped, and a dove cooed in the distance. The girl was not finished. She spoke on, to herself as well as to her companions.

'The poor beast ran away, with two sacks full of relics. It will bless perhaps some peasants who will have very little idea of what they have found.'

She sighed and poked the man in front of her with her staff.

'I'm sure that the donkey had more sense than you, Mathis!'

She left off speaking at this point but her sighs punctuated her uneven steps. The men in front did not answer, but kept walking. It began to drizzle, a fact which did nothing at all for the girl's temper.

'How I wish I had taken father's advice and ...'

She kicked at a protruding rock, stubbed her toe, and almost tripped. She was kept from falling over by the supporting hand of the woman behind her.

'Now then, Marta. Hush you, and be a little more careful. Mathis and Hans have begged their pardon a thousand times already so why must you continually carp? Besides that, it was I who was holding on to the donkey's rope and it was I whose fault it was that the donkey got away.'

The girl turned a surly countenance to the woman who came to walk at her side in spite of the small path.

'Hush yourself, Katrina. They should have chased the beast and brought it back but they were too dull-witted. I have every right to be angry. We lost the relics I paid for dearly in Rome and it was not your fault but mine. I simply should have forbidden them to drink the Rhenish. It was chance that let us stumble across the wedding, and with everyone so hospitable ...'

'Yes,' Katrina interrupted, 'and you could take a lesson there, so free they were with the bread and wine. And was not the groom a welcome host?'

'Yes,' Marta said and stared ahead, suddenly leaning heavily upon her servant, 'he was that. But the whole party probably did very little the whole day and earned not a pfennig.'

'Sometimes there are more important things than pfennigs, will you grant that?'

'I don't know!'

Marta's words wailed like the rain.

'Perhaps you mean that life is more important. But it seems that this life is doing and the eternal life that is held before us seems to swallow up the doing, the ever doing ...'

Her voice trailed off and the party walked on.

Nigh evening, bedraggled and weary, the small group of travellers entered a twisting, rugged forest path. Hans swore he had heard tell of an inn but a kilometre or so into the brush. Although Marta had not much faith in what he said, she and her companions took heart when, after another hour, they saw a faint glim through the trees – light which they very much hoped was the inn Hans had been touting. Pulling, the woollen robe closer about her, she basked in the intermittent brightness as it showed between the wet trees and tried to increase her pace. Marta was in her early twenties, slightly disabled by having been born with a right leg an inch shorter than the left. Keeping her eye on the light, she stumbled over a gnarled and slippery root. The staff slipped from her hand. Katrina caught her waist and, putting her arm about it, supported her. Though the light was not as close as they had initially thought, eventually the foursome reached it. Shaking themselves like cats, Marta knocked on the low-set, wooden door and waited expectantly. Mathis' stomach rumbled.

'Thunder,' he joked and Hans guffawed.

'Hush,' Marta commanded, 'I can hear noise within, and ...'

'... and I smell sausages without,' Hans interrupted which earned him a box on the ears from his mistress.

Marta's knock, which had been rather soft, was not answered and, not caring what his mistress thought, Mathis took it upon himself to use both his fists. Then, when there was still no response, Katrina, upon a nudge by one of the men, carefully tried the latch to see if the door would open. It did and the four found themselves looking into a large and rather musty room. A number of people were sitting on the floor in various corners, children as well as adults, and the hubbub of speech as well as the din of self-absorption, drowned out any awareness of the newcomers.

Marta Reiss, for that was the name of the girl in charge of the party, did not wait to be invited but walked in, Katrina close behind her. The two men quickly followed suit, shutting the door after them. At this point they were noted. There was a lull in the conversation; the newcomers were briefly scrutinized; and then the noise picked up again. The inn, like others in the area, served many and people did not stop to question every person who chanced in through the door.

There was a clay, pot-bellied stove in the centre of the room with a kettle hanging over it. By it sat a stocky woman. Marta, leaving somewhat of a wet trail, walked towards her while the others stayed in the background.

'We've travelled a long distance and wonder if you might have some supper left which we could have?'

'Well, now,' the woman looked Marta up and down, gauging the heavy, serviceable woollen robe held together by a heavy, gold clasp, as well as taking inventory of the rings on her fingers.

'Well, now,' she said again, as a double chin shook and a bulbous wart on her jowls glistened with fat, 'The Cock and Thistle serves from five to seven, and it's long past the hour when I ladled out the food. But perhaps I can reheat some of the sausage and stew which was served this past hour to all these good people here.'

'That would be most kind,' was Marta's reply and turned to find a place in the room in which to sit down.

Katrina had already taken off her cloak and spread it, inside-out, on the rude wooden floor. She beckoned and Marta walked over. The spot was near the door and the only space left which was not occupied with either people or wet clothes. An overpowering odour of damp sweat mingled with garlic and sausage pervaded throughout. Rain pattered down on the roof and Marta, with a sigh, sat herself down next to Katrina. Hans and Mathis sat between them and the door.

'Well, so far so good. I hope that your dear father will not be worried with you not coming home sooner.'

'No, he will not expect us for a week or so,' Marta answered, a trifle more conciliatory now that they were set for the night.

She sighed, adding softly, 'If only he were here as well.'

If the room was not overly clean, at least it was warm. Soon a drowsiness began to steal over the little company who had walked most of that day.

'Where do you hail from?'

To their right a swarthy, rather muscular man addressed Mathis and Hans. His voice was not unfriendly and the seamless robe flung carelessly on the floor next to him had a fur tippet. A velvet cap lay on top of it, a sure sign of wealth.

'From Rome. My mistress was on a pilgrimage. But now we return to Wittenberg.'

Hans always ready to speak, smiled at the fellow who thoughtfully regarded him, repeating the words.

'From Rome back to Wittenberg. A pilgrim, to be sure. A penance imposed on her by her priest, no doubt. And what sin has ...'

He left off speaking. The landlady of the establishment stood before the travellers with four bowls of steaming food.

'There,' she said as she handed down the bowls with wooden spoons, 'and that will cost you extra as you will understand.'

Marta nodded, asking as she took her bowl if they also might have a bit of cup to drink. The woman nodded and was off again.

'To be sure,' the swarthy man spoke again, 'You are all faint for lack of food and drink for you must have been on the road a good many days.'

Hans did not answer as he was now fully concentrated on blowing onto the hot food before easing it into his open mouth. The man left off speaking but did not stop staring, noting that although Marta wore a plain russet gown underneath the woollen robe that now lay discarded at her side, it was edged with intricate lace by the neck. As well, her head-dress, which held a mass of thick, shiny black hair, was an open network of thin gold cording covered with silver stars at the interstices. Marta felt the man's gaze and turned her back towards him feeling quite secure with Hans and Mathis by her side and the trustworthy Katrina right next to her. The landlady soon brought a great mug of beer. It was a dark, muddy colour and smelled dubious. Marta took the mug from her hand, swallowing a small courteous sip, before handing it over to Katrina.

'I thank you,' Marta smiled at the landlady, but the woman had already returned to the stove where she sat down again to oversee her company.

An hour or so later the door opened and bundles of straw were flung in. They were intercepted by the various families and carried over to the places where they had been sitting.

'Our beds,' whispered Katrina, 'and I will get us a mattress as well.'

She stood up and deftly caught a bale under her arm. Plucking it apart, she distributed it on their portion of floor, then lay her cloak on top and bowed to Marta. Marta laughed.

'We will share the straw this night, Katrina and keep one another warm to boot.'

Standing up with some difficulty, her legs stiff from sitting, she hobbled about to help make the bed comfortable.

'You are crippled,' the swarthy man suddenly said, as if he had just discovered it, quickly adding as Marta flushed at the words, 'it matters not whether one is rich or poor, ill fortune comes to all.'

Marta flushed deeper.

'I meant no disre ...'

'Hold your tongue, man,' Katrina lashed out, interrupting him, 'we may be in a poor establishment, but that's no need not to be civil.'

She was barely done speaking when Mathis, who was also fixing his bed and who had heard but half of what was being said, had stood up, shaking his fist under the man's nose.

'You are rude, sir,' he said.

'Mathis!'

Marta's voice was sharp. Mathis was usually a good man, but he had a weakness for drink and lost his temper much too easily. The man laughed heartily. Obviously he had no desire to create ill will. The entire room was paying attention now. Their lives did not hold much excitement and they were always ready for a brawl, a good insult or a lively dialogue.

'I seek no quarrel,' the swarthy man continued, 'and have no wish to wrestle you.'

But Mathis, feeling the eyes of all on him, felt compelled to continue in what he deemed was a defence of Marta's honour. He was a short man, more trained in the art of heavy work than in the art of fighting, and he loudly dared his opponent to stand. Having no choice, the fellow was up in an instant and the next moment saw Mathis on the ground, his nose bleeding, his legs knocked out from under him. Katrina crawling over, tried to staunch the flow of blood with her petticoat. Hans, who had watched the proceedings with trepidation, now stood up as well. He was much younger than Mathis and barely out of boyhood. But before he could do anything, a figure stepped out behind them from the far shadows of the room.

'How now, sir,' a man's voice came through, loud and clear, 'would you attack women and boys? For shame. Take me if you must fight.'

All eyes turned. Marta, red and abashed, saw a middle-aged man standing between her and her swarthy neighbour. Tall and thin, he had an air of confidence about him that could not be mistaken.

'You will not find me dull to fight, sir,' the man continued, 'so why don't we step outside where we won't bother the good folk in this hostel anymore.'

'I had no wish to fight and I still have no wish to fight,' the swarthy man rejoined, 'none at all and I dare say the man whom you call Mathis,' and here he looked directly at Marta, 'will be all right. I did not hit him hard.'

After saying this, he sat down again. His challenger, satisfied that he would no longer bother anyone, turned and bowed to Marta.

'Erlin Von Reicht at your service, my lady.'

Marta smiled and offered him her hand.

'Marta Reiss,' she said.

He studied her face almost as if he were recalling something, before he took hold of her hand, kissed it and smiled back.

'You are a beautiful young lady, Marta Reiss, and I count it an honour to have been of service to you.'

'Thank you, I ...'

She stopped abruptly. Out of the corner of her eye she saw that the swarthy man had crawled to where Mathis lay on the straw, nursing his jaw with his hand. Before either Katrina or Hans could stop him, the man had bent his head over Mathis and had whispered something into his ear. Cursing under his breath, Erlin moved aside, kicking the figure.

'Back, sir! Go back to where you came from!'

Turning to the landlady, he gestured that she should come over, even as the swarthy man edged back to his spot.

'Ursula, this man should not be allowed to stay. He molests your guests and will give your inn a bad name.'

The landlady slowly moved her bulk over. Her rotund face did not look pleased and the hairs on her wart trembled.

'I reckon you best be off, Elias,' she said, her voice rougher than the rafters on the ceiling, 'and you'd best not hang about or I'll set my dogs on you.'

Elias grimaced, bent over to pick up his robe and cap, and winked at Marta before giving Mathis a long, penetrating gaze. His back was towards Erlin von Reicht, but both Marta and Katrina could see that he mouthed something to Mathis.

'Out then! Don't dally!'

The landlady's voice, strident and harsh, caused some of the younger children to move closer to their parents. Elias picked up his bag, pulled on his velvet cap and cape, bowed and opened the door. It had almost stopped raining and, unaccountably, Marta was glad even though she was relieved that the man would be gone. When the door closed behind him, she sighed. Almost immediately, the noise from the other travellers increased. It was as if Elias had never been in the room at all.

It was some twenty minutes later that the landlady slid off her seat once more and came over to Marta.

'Everything to your lady's liking?

'Yes.'

Marta's reply was short and curt. She did not care for the woman and had no desire to become involved in trite conversation.

'I have a room upstairs which has a bed which might be more comfortable for yourself and your friends.'

Marta looked at the woman distrustfully. Why had she not mentioned this before? But the thought of a bed and some privacy was tempting. She looked at Katrina who shrugged wearily. The candles on the table flickered and the hoarse snoring of several of those already asleep assailed her ears.

'Very well,' she assented.

Getting up with difficulty, she followed the landlady to the far corner of the room. There, in a small annex, was a steep, straight staircase. Ursula swung a lantern with her right hand, handed Katrina and Marta a candle and made her way up ahead of the party. Shadows played back and forth and something akin to fear prickled Marta's skin. The woman's body odour drifted down, falling on her like a curse. Behind her she could hear Hans and Mathis whispering. Their familiar voices calmed her. They carried their straw pallets as well as their bundles and yawned simultaneously.

'Here it is.'

There was only one door at the top of the staircase. Creaking and groaning on its wooden hinges, it sent shivers down Marta's spine. All four followed Ursula in. There was a large window to the left, and Marta was glad of it, for all that the moon was scarce to be seen and the sky full of clouds. There was comfort in the space and odd easement in glimpses of the sky.

'Here, as you see, is the bed.'

It was an old bed with an iron casing around it. The landlady lifted her lantern, smiling obsequiously the whole time, all five of her teeth visible. Then she waited. Katrina coughed discreetly, behind her hand. Marta knew what she was thinking. The covers on the bed had a mouldy tinge to them, even as the flaking iron bars on the bed were brown.

'It'll do you fine, you'll see,' Ursula said, sidling back to the door.

Hans and Mathis let her through. And then she was gone.

'Well,' Hans said, as soon as the door closed, 'at least we won't have to deal with any more unruly neighbours tonight.'

Mathis nursed his bruised nose and scowled. Walking over to the window, he deposited his straw on another heap of straw that was already lying under the window ledge.

'I trow we'll have enough straw here, Hans, to keep us comfortable.'

'Don't be too quick about that,' Katrina intervened.

She had thrown back the coverlet and both she and Marta could see the mattress move. 'Lice,' Katrina whispered, throwing the cover back on, 'We'll be sleeping on the floor next to you fellows. I don't fancy lying down in there.'

'Nor I,' Marta whispered back, 'and I think perhaps we should bar the door if we could, for I do not know ...'

They all looked at each other.

'The woman was trustworthy, I think,' Hans said slowly, hopefully, 'she winked at me as she left ...'

'Oh, you great goose,' Katrina remonstrated with him, 'go on with you and you still wet behind the ears.'

'Well,' Mathis said as he scratched his back, 'perhaps we can move the bed in front of the door and if Hans and I lie behind it and if you both lie by the window, I think we should all wake should something happen ...'

He left of speaking and moved towards the bed. Hans, followed suit. They both pulled and shoved and tugged the foot of the bed, but could not budge the piece.

'Shall I help?' Katrina said, and Marta, in spite of her weariness, smiled.

'And I?' she added.

'Tis stuck,' Hans panted, 'or has some boulders wedged in the mattress.'

Mathis left off pulling and went down on his hands and knees.

'Give me some light, Katrina,' he panted, 'perhaps there's something under the bed holding it in place.'

She knelt down next to him, and he cursed.

'Watch your tongue, sir,' she cried, 'that will not do at all! And our mistress returning from a pilgrimage. Will not the Virgin Mary herself be angry with you!?'

Mathis paid her no heed but went on talking excitedly.

'The foot of the bed is tacked to the floor. See Hans, it is clamped down like a ... like ... well, I don't know what it is clamped down like ... but I have never seen anything like it. It's not as if someone would want to steal this piece of junk.'

'It is not clamped down at the head, Mathis,' said Hans, who knelt down next to him and looked as well, 'Just at the foot. Well, I suppose they are worried that some folk might rob ...'

'Rob?' Katrina entered the conversation with gusto, 'What is there to rob in here? That is a sillier statement than seeing a windmill in a desert. Of course,' she added, after a pause, 'there is the matter of Marta's purse ...'

She left off speaking.

'Well,' Marta said, 'why-ever the bed is tacked to the floor, it is so and we must let the bed stay in its place. Perhaps, Mathis and Hans you will be so good as to sleep at the door's threshold, so that we need not be surprised should someone come to wake us suddenly.'

Getting up, the men moved a portion of the straw in front of the door and lay down. Katrina and Marta followed suit under the window sill, after first putting Katrina's cloak overtop of the straw and spreading Marta's cloak over them as a blanket.

They had lain down for only an hour or so, when, unaccountably Marta's eyes were drawn to the window. She had heard something, or perhaps she had dreamt something. There was more light now and she could see stars and the moon between the swiftly moving clouds. Next to her, Katrina breathed heavily and both Hans and Mathis snored companionably. Then all woke, for a sound like that of heavy metal striking another piece of metal vibrated through the room. Katrina grabbed Marta's body and began to say a Hail Mary.

'Shh,' Marta whispered, 'I'm all right and whatever the sound was, it has stopped.'

She loosened herself from Katrina's hold and sat up. The moon and the stars were as they had been a moment ago. Over the beating of her heart, she moved her head to regard the place where Mathis and Hans lay. She could see the whites of their eyes glisten as they too were sitting up.

'The bed, mistress,' whispered Mathis, 'look at the bed. It's gone.'

Marta turned her head and some two feet over, where the bed had been, there was nothing – nothing except the iron footing. Blackness, cavernous and devilish, gaped where the floor had been. Pulling her robe around her, Marta inched over to the hole and peered into the darkness. It was so thick she felt she could write in it with her finger. Was that what purgatory looked like? Mindful of the fragility of her own life, her hand moved up into the warmth of her robe. The clasp, loosely set into the upper folds, fell out and disappeared into the abyss. After what seemed like an eternity, she could hear it land with a small clink. She backed up to where she had been lying down with Katrina.

'I forgot to tell you,' Mathis whispered from by the door, 'that the man who was named Elias warned me that you should not do as the landlady should bid you.'

'When did he tell you that?' Marta whispered back.

'When he crawled over just before this Erlin von Reicht kicked him. He also tried to tell me something else just before he was ordered out. But I couldn't quite understand what he was mouthing.'

Katrina, pulling herself up by the window sill, stood up and spoke in a low voice.

'Whoever it was that caused the bed to drop, will be checking to see if we are ... if we are ...'

She stopped.

'Dead,' Marta finished.

'But they knew we would not all be ...' Hans contributed.

'Right,' Katrina said, 'and I think that they will be checking up on this room soon. But not until after the guests have all gone will they act. I'll warrant the door is locked on the outside and that ...'

'Shh,' Mathis said and put his finger on his lips.

They all froze and heard footsteps, the tiniest of footsteps, coming up the stairs.

'Snore,' Marta ordered Mathis and Hans, 'snore – and do it now.'

Hans lay down immediately and began to breathe heavily. Mathis followed suit. Their harsh breathing carried over into snoring, and Katrina and Marta both saw the soft light of a candle flicker underneath the door. Katrina, who had sat down again, pinched Marta's hand so hard she almost cried out. And then, just as quietly as it had come, the light disappeared. Mathis and Hans snored another full two minutes before being stopped by the women. Then they sat up again and grinned at one another. A moment later, all four crawled over to where the bed had been. They could make out very little.

'We should leave before light,' Hans said weakly.

'We should leave now,' Katrina said.

'But how? Have you looked out the window? It's too high to jump.'

Marta put her head into her hands to think. Mathis fumbled about with his bag and opened it. Drawing out a sturdy rope, he dangled it triumphantly before them all.

'It's a rope ... oh, Mathis, I will never be cross with you anymore.'

Marta almost laughed in her joy.

Mathis, sheepish in pride, grumbled, 'I've carried it with me a long time, and should the donkey's rope have broken, well ... I would have been ready.'

'Never mind what you would have done, Mathis! Tie it to the iron bedpost now,' Katrina said, 'It should hold. We certainly couldn't move it when we tried before.'

Marta moved to the window to assess the drop. It was almost twenty-five feet down to the ground. There was not much growth – just some grass and then the forest next to it.

'How long is that rope, Mathis?'

'Not long enough, I warrant. But if we throw the straw down,' he answered from where he stood tying the rope up securely, 'we should land well and be able to manage.'

Hans went down first, hand over hand. When he reached the end of the rope, he let go, dropping with a small thud onto the heap of straw. It rustled a bit, but for all that there was no noise but that of a night owl hooting in the distance. Katrina went down next. Bravely her body strained and bravely she lowered herself until Hans told her to let go and fall free. Marta, watching from the window, could see that she closed her eyes and obeyed almost immediately. Her skirt ballooned out a bit, and softened the twelve feet of free fall. Landing next to and falling against Hans, she seemed to be unhurt.

'You next, my lady,' Mathis said, and helped Marta onto the sill, holding her under the arms until she had a firm grasp on the rope. Hand over hand, she went down as well. But when she reached the end of the cord, she was afraid to let go.

'Marta,' Katrina whispered, 'I will catch you. We will both catch you, Hans and I. Just trust us.'

Marta looked up. Mathis stared down at her from the casement of the window. His face was white in the moonlight.

'If you don't go down,' he said, 'I will not be able to get down and I think I hear voices on the stairs again.'

She nodded imperceptibly, and let go, almost swooning with the effort and the next moment found herself lying on top of Katrina who, after a moment, disentangled herself and enveloped Marta in a bear hug. Then Mathis was standing next to them. Eyeing the window, he whispered urgently.

'We must be off into the woods before they catch sight of us. Didn't the woman Ursula say she had dogs?'

'But,' Katrina countered, as they all began to follow his form in the direction of the forest, 'surely she will not try that until all her guests have gone.'

'That could be,' Mathis said, 'but we'll not take the chance. I'm not so sure of the direction, though ...'

'Maybe you'll permit myself ...?'

All four jumped, Katrina and Marta crying out softly in alarm. Elias, the man who had sat next to them in the inn, stood behind them.

'Please forgive me for startling you. I've been waiting for sometime and hope you will permit me to escort you through the woods towards the main road ... to Wittenberg, I believe?'

No one replied. Everyone stared at him. His camel-coloured cloak with its fur tippet glistened in the moonlight. His eyes, dark and twinkling, looked straight at Marta. The velvet cap perched jauntily on his head.

'Look here, uh ...'

Mathis could not recall the fellow's name.

'Elias. Elias Wasser, to be exact. I'm sorry, you have had such an unpleasant experience but I am delighted that you have escaped the clutches of The Cock and Thistle. But we mustn't hang about. If she does not find you in your room, she will, no doubt, set her dogs on you as well as ...'

He stopped.

'Who are you?'

Katrina had finally found her tongue and she cast a hostile look at the man. He returned her gaze evenly, and she found his grey eyes a little disconcerting. At the same time she instinctively trusted the man even before he replied.

'I'm a traveller, as you are. I've had dealings with this inn and have heard stories. That is why I tried to get the attention of your man here, Mathis, I believe, to tell him not to do what the landlady told you and to keep your wits about you.'

'That's true,' Hans said, 'he did so tell you, Mathis. For so you told us later in the room but only after the bed ...'

Mathis scratched his head. A dog bayed, not too far off.

'We must be going,' Elias said, 'and we must walk fast.

He took a leather belt from his satchel handing the front end to Mathis.

'Hold on to my cloak with your right hand, man, and hold the belt with your left. Give Marta the other end of the belt. And you, Katrina, grab hold of Marta's robe. That's right! Now, follow me!'

Tightly Marta held on to her end of the belt. Her robe, in turn, was grasped by Katrina. Hans made up the rear and seemed to be able to follow without any problem. Elias seemed to know where he was going and remembering that Marta was lame, walked not overly fast, but always north – north towards Wittenberg. Finally, when the sun was rising in the east and the forest much thinner than it had been, he permitted them all to sit down and rest. Marta was very tired. They were in a small glade. Leaning against a mossy tree stump, she fell asleep almost immediately, not wakening or being wakened until the sun was much higher in the sky. First she was confused, but then she remembered and turned her head to look for their benefactor.

'Where is Elias?'she asked the others who were awake already, putting her arms above her head in a luxurious stretch.

'He left as soon as you and Katrina fell asleep,' Mathis answered, 'and bid us farewell for a while. He is off to buy more provisions. We will see him later today. We are to take you to the road which we see from where we sit. He said that it ought to take us in the direction of Wittenberg.'

'Oh,' was all Marta could manage.

'He left us some food as well. A manchet of bread and a flask of wine mixed with water. He bade me tell you to think of it as a gift.'

The whole affair puzzled them greatly. While they were partaking of the bread and the wine, Mathis also told Marta that Elias had advised them to steer clear of the next town, to bypass it if they could, perhaps in a roundabout route.

'Why?' Katrina asked.

'He said the folk were not too friendly,' Mathis replied, 'and that to avoid trouble we should be better off ...'

He left off speaking and shrugged, indicating that he really had no idea as to why.

When they began their journey again, Katrina talked of nothing else but Erlin von Reicht and Elias Wasser as the party made its way north toward Northeim and then Wittenberg. Katrina favoured Erlin but she was also impressed with the fact that Elias had led them through the forest.

'He is a true blood,' she avowed, as they trudged along, 'and did you ever see two such grey eyes in a countenance so noble? I'll warrant he is related to a baron or some such personage.'

'Oh, hush, Katrina,' Hans said, 'you see nobility in a raven and all he does is caw.'

'He did more than caw,' Katrina answered crossly, 'and he certainly helped us at a desperate time. As well, he warned us about the danger of accepting the landlady's hospitality, an advice, I might add, which we didn't hear until it was too late. And all I can say,' she added, 'is that Mathis is, no doubt, the clumsiest oaf all the year 1517 has seen.'

'Oh, Katrina,' Marta said, 'yesterday you bade me not to be harsh with Mathis. Now you yourself must leave off teasing him. He protected well and would have risen to the occasion, as actually he did, if not this Elias Wasser had stepped forward.'

Mathis puffed out his chest and began to whistle. He loved his mistress Marta and basked in her praise. They bypassed the first town, as Elias had advised and walked until noon. By that time they had reached a small city, replete with walls and gates. The sky was blue and gone were the storm clouds they had encountered the day before.

'There is no sign of Elias, so perhaps he will not come back. But we should be able to buy some bread and wine here ourselves,' Marta said, trying to keep disappointment out of her voice, 'and perhaps we can also find someone who might give us directions to Wittenberg.'

'It was a shame about losing the donkey, and I confess again that it was my fault,' Katrina sighed, 'or we might have been further on already. But then,' she went on, casting a sly glance at Marta, 'Erlin von Reicht would not have had the chance to kiss your lily-white hand.'

'Oh, stop it,' was all Marta would say, 'and did not Father Stenck say the pilgrimage would be more efficacious if we went on foot and carried everything on our backs? So perhaps this last part of the journey will be more ...'

'But Father Stenck also advised you to enter a nunnery.'

Katrina frowned as she interrupted.

'And I ...'

She stopped because down the street leading out from the gate, a group of people, subdued and silent, walked towards them. At the head of the group was a man whom they all recognized to be Erlin von Reicht. Only he appeared different from when they had seen him the night before. His thin form now wore a monk's cowl and a black robe flapped about him.

Marta moved to the side of the road. The others followed suit and in a few minutes the crowd reached them. Erlin's eye had caught sight of them and he held up his hand. Then everyone stopped.

'Marta Reiss.'

Erlin's voice sounded unfamiliar and grating. His call was not a greeting as much as it was a command.

'I missed you this morning when I left the inn.'

Marta did not know how to reply. To tell him, and the entire crowd that she had escaped through a window and that the bed had disappeared, seemed rather silly in broad daylight.

'You are a pilgrim,' Erlin's voice went on, 'and I trow you would gain much benefit from watching a thief hang.'

'A thief?'

'Indeed to watch an unrepentant thief hang and to call him back to the arms of Mother Church, is a step closer to paradise.'

'A thief?' Marta repeated rather dully.

It was only then that she saw the cage on a low cart at the back of the group. The cart was being pulled by an ox. And in the cage, face averted, sat Elias Wasser. Erlin kept talking.

'After the man is hung, I shall return to the village to await the coming of John Diezel. Commissioned by the archbishop and carrying the pope's bull, I shall help him sell indulgences.'

Marta's feet were rooted to the ground. She heard very little of what Erlin was saying but saw only the cage. Tightening her hold on her staff, she felt Mathis tense next to her.

'What has the man stolen?'

'A clasp – a golden clasp.'

Erlin reached into his black garb and took something out.

'I trow you will recognize it!'

He held up a brooch, fashioned from gold and shaped like an R. Instinctively her hand moved up to where the brown robe came together at her throat.

'It is not there, is it?'

'I lost it yesterday.'

Her answer was hesitant, her mind muddled. But then it cleared. She knew she had still had the brooch in the room; and that it had dropped into the darkness below. How could Elias have taken it? It could only have been taken by someone who had been involved with the landlady in getting rid of wayfarers.

'The clasp was not lost but stolen,' Erlin said loudly, holding it up for all to see, 'and when I saw this base fellow carry it about in your fair city, a fellow who bothered this pilgrim but yesterday at the inn, I thought it only right to execute justice. Harbouring a miscreant, as you all know, impedes the salvation of a town and of all the souls who have died in it previously. Therefore, to help you good people, I apprehended him and ...'

'Have you had the bailiff oversee the matter?' Marta interrupted him.

Katrina gripped Marta's hand as she was speaking, shaking it as if she were shaking her head at Marta's words.

Erlin stood immediately in front of Marta. He was not so fine as she had thought last night. If he had not seen her leave the inn why had he not gone to check to see where she was?

'These good people,' Erlin said, 'are the judges. They helped me apprehend the man and now they, as well as God's law, demand justice. Is that not so, my good folk?'

A murmur ran through the crowd.

'Where is the bailiff?'

Marta persisted but her heart was beating fast. Surely the man Elias was not a felon. And why had Erlin not worn a priest's garb last night. It was on the tip of her tongue to ask, but when she looked at his gaunt face, cold, impassive and somehow greedy, she swallowed the words. It was best not to antagonize him. A child in the crowd answered her question.

'The bailiff is just behind us. He had some business to attend to and will be coming presently.'

'Indeed,' Erlin said, 'and we now go on to the creek to erect the gibbet. All those for Mother Church and her purity and salvation, follow me.'

He bowed formally to Marta, adding, 'I hope to see you later, Marta Reiss.'

Marta stepped aside and the group moved on. Katrina pulled at Marta's robe.

'Let's go! Let's not stay here!'

Marta bit her lip. Elias had warned Mathis, had led them through the forest, and now this. Was Erlin a surrogate priest or a shyster? Staring at the disappearing crowd, she could still make out Elias' back. His cloak was gone and his velvet cap. A leather jerkin covered his bare back and a thin trail of dried blood covered his arms. He had never once looked up.

'They have judged him quickly,' she whispered.

'Come!' Katrina whispered urgently, still pulling at her cloak.

'Were it not the best pilgrimage of all to do right?' Marta answered.

'Come, my dear! We need not watch or wait! What a horror there will be! Come!'

But Marta would not be moved. She watched the retreating group, remembering how Elias Wasser had come to her aid in leading them all through the forest. Why had he done that?

'I will stop it,' she murmured to herself, but loud enough for all to hear, and then 'At least I will try.'

'You cannot,' Katrina was aghast, 'Speak out for this Elias, this man whom we only met yesterday, and you will swing next to him. Cannot you feel it?'

'You described him as a noble only this morning, Katrina.'

'Yes, but then he was not in a cage.'

'There is the bailiff,' Hans said.

A squat man ran down the street, his woollen cap askew and his face flushed. In no time he had reached them and would have run by but for the fact that Marta stepped in front of him so as to almost make him bump into her.

'Sir,' she cried out loudly, 'Sir, a moment of your time, if you please.'

'I cannot,' he huffed, 'I have to ...'

'Yes, I know,' she answered, 'and that is why I must speak with you.'

He had come to a full stop and heaving in the chest, made as if to go on.

'I know yon man whom you intend to hang,' Marta said boldly, 'and you make a great mistake for he is no thief.'

'If he is no thief, why had he the gold brooch on his person? The priest said it belonged to a pilgrim who had lodged with him at an inn but yesterday.'

'I am the pilgrim. It was my brooch but, ... that is to say, I gave it to him as a token of my ... of my affection.'

And all the while, Katrina, Mathis and Hans stood behind Marta ready to bolt if necessary.

'My name is Marta Reiss. You may know my father, I think,' Marta went on, 'He is one of the merchants in Wittenberg who deals in wheat and linens, as well as pottery and other merchandise. I believe you have done business with him.'

She stopped and as she fingered her money belt he left off loud breathing for a moment.

'Reiss?' he said after a moment, and again, 'Reiss?'

'Yes,' she smiled, undoing the leather belt hanging from her waist, 'and I do believe that we could come to an agreement. But you must be swift and stop the hanging.'

'I don't know,' he hesitated, 'to vouch for the man is one thing, but to explain to the pardoner is another. The arm of the church has long fingernails and scratches so that it draws blood. The priest, who is a pardoner, has promised indulgences to all who will watch the hanging.'

He stopped and considered, looking longingly at the pouch on the leather belt. She shook some gold from it into her palm.

'The man is my betrothed,' she said, 'and I will make it worth your while. Keep the brooch for all I care. But tell the crowd it was put on his person by a mischief-maker and that he is clean and on his way to a betrothal feast in Wittenberg.'

Fascinated by the glitter in her palm, the bailiff slowly extended his hand. Making a fist over the coins that Marta slowly dropped into his palm, he nodded and betook himself to running again. Marta, Katrina, Hans and Mathis gazed after him.

'There is a Goliath untruth,' Katrina ventured when he was out of earshot, 'and what shall we do when the black sheep comes bleating home?'

'We shall take him in,' Marta said firmly, 'and you shall all back me up when the angry burghers of this small place come back.'

'Yes, mistress,' Hans answered eagerly, 'so we shall. I for one ... I for one ...'

And then he fell silent, for thinking about it was a very difficult matter.

* * *

Lazar Reiss had been born and bred in Wittenberg. Descended from a long line of landed gentry who owned property around Wittenberg, he had the privilege of Ausbürgertum, of associate citizenship. Lazar owned a rather large estate in the city and although he could easily have lived on the rents, dues and interests of various investments, he chose to keep active in merchandise. He bought and sold and kept busy in trade and banking. His only regret was that he had no son to follow him. Although he loved Marta dearly, he was worried that she would not be able to manage without him. In spite of the fact that she had a considerable dowry that would accompany her upon marriage, there had been no takers – no takers to suit him, that is. There were always fortune hunters on the horizon and they were not acceptable. Besides that there was the matter, even though she was a handsome young woman, of her crippled leg; and a second cause of concern was that she was half-Jewish. Lazar was not a practicing Jew. But neither did he reject his heritage. On the whole, the Reisses were tolerated in Wittenberg society. They were known to be honest people and ones who treated their servants well. In spite of this fact, Lazar was well aware that other German palatinates might not accept them. If ever a city was subject to famine or plague or some other disaster, it was not at all uncommon for the Jewish population to be blamed. He knew, for example, that nearly two hundred Jews had been burned alive in Strasbourg in 1349.

'It was more than one hundred and fifty years ago, I know,' he had told Marta, 'but people must always have someone to blame and there are many towns, many cities, many stories and ... many Jews. We are, little girl, a scapegoat.'

For this reason Lazar never sought either a social or a political spotlight, preferring instead to dwell quietly with his family and a few trusted servants. But he did wish the girl were married to someone who would protect her. His wife had been Catholic and that was how Marta had been raised. She was a pious girl, even as his wife had been a pious woman, but both Marta and Maria mistrusted the priests and monks who ministered in the local church.

Maria Reiss had died last year of a fever. Her illness had come up so quickly that there had been no time, no time at all, to call a priest or to say goodbye. Marta had been frantic with worry about her mother's immortal soul. When, after spending days on her knees at church, the priest had suggested a pilgrimage to Rome, more than five hundred miles away, he had protested. Surely there had to be a closer place for a pilgrimage, if there had to be a pilgrimage. But almost ill with grief, Marta would not listen to him. The priest, a Father Stenck, who had also been a distant cousin of his wife, had further suggested that the purchase of relics for the church in Wittenberg would go a long way towards moving a soul out of purgatory, especially a soul who had not received the last rites.

'Besides that,' Father Stenck had lectured a subdued Marta, 'the indulgences purchased in Rome have greater efficacy than those here in Saxony. As well, in Rome you can confess, for your mother as well as for yourself, and so lighten your soul. In that city you can make your soul as clean as it was right after your baptism.'

'And my mother's soul?' she had cried.

'There is a saying in Rome,' Father Stenck had responded, 'blessed is the mother whose daughter celebrates a mass in St. Giovanni in Laterano on a Saturday.'

'I will do it,' Marta answered.

'And child,' the priest went on, 'scale the steps of La Scala on your knees, with an Our Father on each step, for by praying this way you will also bring her closer to heaven.'

Marta had left. There had been no stopping her even though Lazar had tried. She had agreed to take Hans and Mathis, two of his male servants. Katrina, an older servant who had been with the family for years, had volunteered to go along as well.

It was some two months after Marta's departure that the plague had come to the area in and around Wittenberg. Three of Lazar's servants died in quick succession and the remaining four bolted overnight – fled the house – and he did not know what had become of them. Streets were empty and he chose not to go about much. He could see the smoke of fires from his chair by the window of his study on the third floor of the house – fires which had been lighted for the purification of the air. Like himself very few ventured about on the streets save the men who, with carts and coffins, came to fetch corpses. In this manner he became aware that his neighbours had perished. The continuous tolling of the church bells, interspersed with the cawing and croaking of ravens, was ominous. He thought much on death and dying and wondered more about his mortal soul than he had ever wondered before. God had struck Israel with a plague in the desert and it had been for disobeying Him. That much he knew. It was on the fourth day after the servants had left that Lazar knew for a fact that he had also contracted the dread disease. There was painful swelling under his armpits and he must now come face to face with what he had been thinking about these past few days. And what about his daughter, what about Marta who would become an orphan upon his demise. Wearily climbing the stairs to the third floor, Lazar sat down at his desk and wrote:

My dearly beloved daughter:

Although I know not how it is in the rest of the city, our own street, as I write you this letter, is almost deserted. The occasional cart still passes through but the plague is playing her death dance and few remain to step to her tune. I saw Herr Stauff yesterday without a cloak, carrying wood on his back, head bent, arms dangling. And that was the man who aspired to be a member of the City Council but last summer. Dogs and cats walk abroad boldly as if they own the road and I have seen some of them chewing on what appears to be human remains. If there is one blessing in this whole accursed situation, it is that you, dear daughter are not with me at this time.

As I write this I know that I too shall soon be no more. Do not reproach yourself for leaving me. Rest assured that I am content to go. I have tried to pray these last days. Yes, your old profligate father who scorned your and your mother's religion – he tried to pray. But not to those stone idols, those lifeless statues to whom you always genuflect out of fear for not doing something right. But enough!! I would be content if I knew that you were safe. I am putting the deed to our summer home in Salzburg in this envelope. It is in your name. And I buried, this morning, the strong box with the gold in it by our secret spot. Beware unless that black-robed raven who calls himself your mother's cousin, should get his hands on your inheritance. I trust he will try when he finds out I am ill. Never, Marta, never become a nun as he will most certainly try to persuade you to become should I die! Worry not for my soul, child! Worry not!

Now, how to get this to you. I know not, I truly know not. For this my miserable condition prevents me from being able to walk far. But if I find someone, I shall endeavour to print his name on the edge of the paper so that you shall know it came indeed by my hand.

Your devoted father,

Lazar Reiss

After Lazar had written this letter, he meticulously folded it, as well as the deed of which he had written, into an envelope and then made his way out of the study and down the winding staircase. Clutching the envelope in his hand, he crossed the foyer, made his way to the front door, opened it and walked out without bothering to shut the door behind him. On the street he was all concentration on finding someone, anyone to deliver the letter to Marta. The boils under his armpits were large and hard and he was incredibly thirsty. The doors and windows of most of the houses he passed on the street were nailed up and Lazar decided to make for the church. Perhaps someone there, not corrupted by the greed which was so rampant, would help. He managed the several blocks to the cathedral in half delirium. Eventually reaching the steps, he attempted to climb up but was repulsed by several men who brandished swords at him and told him to leave.

'Get yourself to the pest-house, old man,' they shouted, 'Leave, and do not come near us with your infected carcass.'

He stumbled down again, bewildered. His head ached and suddenly his body gave way. Moaning, he fell, hitting his head on the bottom step with a resounding smack. And through a small side-window of the church, eyes keenly observed Lazar as he lay on the road totally oblivious of his surroundings.

When Lazar came to he found himself on a bed in a small room, he knew not where, a strange, dark-haired man sitting by his side. When the stranger noted that he had opened his eyes, he dipped a cloth into a bowl of water and gently wet his lips.

'Here you go, sir. I am sorry to have no wine or beer, but as it is these commodities are presently difficult to come by.'

'Who are you?'

Lazar had not the presence of mind for formalities and came straight to the point.

'A student of the University of Wittenberg.'

Lazar stared at him, trying to remember his circumstances. He said nothing for a while and then half-sat up.

'Why,' he asked, 'are you helping me? Are you a priest?'

The fellow laughed.

'Heaven forbid,' he chuckled, 'for then I should not be here.'

'Indeed,' muttered Lazar, falling back into the sheets which embraced him with their wonderful coolness, 'you should not.'

He closed his eyes. Then, suddenly and frantically, he felt about for his letter.

'What is it?'

The younger man bent over him.

'My letter. I had a letter.'

'So you did and there it is.'

The student pointed to a nearby table and Lazar saw his envelope, crumpled and smeared with dirt.

'I must have ... I must have it!'

The fellow stood up, took the letter from the table and put it into Lazar's hands. He pulled the document under the sheets, clutching it to his bosom, closing his eyes for a moment before opening them wide again, fastening them on his benefactor. Then he spoke, his thoughts threading together incoherently.

'Will you give this letter to my daughter? She will be alone and ... she is lame. Please, will you ...?'

He left off speaking, exhausted.

'Surely.'

The answer was resolute and not long in coming.

'I am dying. Why are you not afraid to be near me?'

'My whole family died of the plague. I think, for some reason, God makes me immune to the disease.'

Lazar felt very weary and longed to go to sleep. But he wanted very much to explain his dilemma.

'I have no time to ... to gauge the vices as well as the virtues which you seem to have. Every man ... every man has both. But you appear very kind. What is your name?'

'You must rest, sir. Don't worry. I will stay with you.'

Determined Lazar sat up again.

'My daughter's inheritance is at stake. There is someone else who might want to ... But what is your name?'

'Elias, sir. Elias Wasser.'

'Have you a pen, Elias? I must write a ... a postscript on this letter.'

A few moments later Lazar, supported by Elias, had added in the margin of the letter:

... daughter, this man is to be trusted and his name is Elias Wasser.'

* * *

In the shadowed confines of a small chamber in the bailiff's house, Marta faced Elias Wasser as he sat across from her at a wooden table. The bailiff stood in a corner of the room, a room lighted only by a narrow window covered by vertical iron bars. The man, who had identified himself as Gerard Pontius, nervously gazed out at the street.

'I have jeopardized my position,' he said, his back to them, 'by intervening with the pardoner and I am certain that one of the pope's own men will soon come to our city.'

'One of the pope's own men? Whatever do you mean?'

Elias spoke softly but clearly, eyeing the bailiff as he turned and wrung his hands in obvious distress.

'Have you not heard of John Diezel? He has been commissioned by the Archbishop of Mainz to travel through Germany and yon pardoner, Erlin von Reicht is merely waiting here to meet up with the man. We were sent word last week that he would be here today.'

As both Marta and Elias shook their heads, he continued.

'Diezel is better known as Tetzel.'

'And what is he to us?' Marta exclaimed angrily.

She saw that Elias was in pain and needed care and it irked her that the bailiff extended no help beyond the fact that he had promised the crowd and an irate Erlin von Reicht that he would investigate the matter.

'Once Diezel, or Tetzel, is here,' the bailiff's voice quivered nervously, 'I don't know what the people will believe and I will no longer be able to protect you.'

'Or yourself, you mean! You coward!' Marta spit out, 'You took my gold without any twinges of conscience. Will a little more ward off the fear of ...'

She stopped. Elias lifted his hand, motioning that she leave off speaking. He stood up, scraping his chair backwards over the tiled floor and walked over to the bailiff.

'We will leave this place and you can say we have escaped.'

Mathis and Hans, who stood in the open doorway with Katrina between them, looked at one another doubtfully.

'It is near certain,' the bailiff said, 'that is to say, we have it on good authority, that Tetzel will arrive later today.'

'What is it you want us to do?' Elias asked.

'I want you to leave, and to leave immediately. But before you do,' and he stopped and wrung his hands together again, 'I want you to hit me hard so that I will be able to show that I tried to stop you – that I tried to prevent you from escaping.'

'Hit you?' Elias repeated.

'Yes,' the bailiff concurred eagerly, 'and take the clasp as well. I will say you took it from me.'

He held out the clasp to Marta who took it from his outstretched hand before passing it back to Katrina.

'I cannot steal,' she commented wryly, 'what belongs to me, Gerard Pontius.'

'There is a path behind this building,' the bailiff went on, unperturbed by her disdain, 'and it will take you north in a roundabout way. You will eventually come out on the road you were on as you were travelling into town. But first you will come to a small green door in the city wall. It is open. Go through and continue on the path. It bypasses the city gates and leads you to the road. After a kilometre or so you will pass a clump of elm trees set together on the right hand side of the road. They are a singular group of trees and you cannot help but notice them. Behind these trees are some bushes and behind these bushes is a path of sorts which leads through a field. After another kilometre there is an old hut where you might spend the night. It is not commonly known. Stay there, a day or two,' he went on, looking askance as Elias, 'to get your wind. I have put enough viands into a bag for you so that you will not suffer hunger.'

'Running away will only seem to prove guilt,' Marta said.

Elias thoughtfully rubbed his chin with his right hand.

'Yet the bailiff is right. As I said, I have heard of this Tetzel. I did not know his name was also Diezel. Is he not the son of a goldsmith in Leipzig and is he not a Dominican monk?

'He is the one.'

The bailiff confirmed Elias' words by nodding vigorously.

'There was a scandal about him of some sort and I heard at one time that he had been convicted of a crime. Indeed, that he had been sentenced to be put into a sack and drowned. But in the end he was obviously not put into a sack. It seems friends in high places tend to help a person escape moral law, in this life anyway. Now it is rumoured abroad that he will make a great show of carrying a red cross which bears the arms of the pope, as he comes into Saxon cities and towns. It is also said that he is selling indulgences to all who will pay – indulgences for the living as well as for the dead.'

'Well, what of it?' Marta said, 'that proves nothing to anyone about you, Elias Wasser.'

'No, but Erlin von Reicht will be sure to put in a bad word about both of us and given Tetzel's influence, I think it would be better if we met neither of them again on this side of the grave,' Elias replied.

Marta stared at him for a long while.

'Perhaps,' Elias said, not at all discomfited and staring back at her, 'you wish to stay and listen to Tetzel yourself? Perhaps you wish to buy his indulgences?'

Marta's eyes filled with tears.

'I know not,' she whispered, 'I know not. But I do know that I do not trust Erlin von Reicht. Corruption surrounds him like the black cloak he wears and I've no stomach for it. And any friend of his I am not likely to trust either. So we are agreed then, I think, that we should leave this place.'

Moving towards the door, she asked for Elias' cape and cap and the bailiff pointed to a hook on the wall behind the door where indeed his garments were hanging. Mathis stepped forward.

'Can I hit the bailiff?' he requested, looking first at Marta and then at Elias.

'Why not,' Elias shrugged, 'it is what he wants. Although,' and he turned and faced the man again, 'you are free to come with us, sir. Why not leave here, for a while anyway?'

The bailiff's eyes flickered.

'No, I was born and bred here and besides, I seek to buy an indulgence for my son. He died at this time last year. He was thirteen.'

Elias sighed.

'Stay then. God has used you to help us, sir, and I thank you for it.'

Mathis came and stood in front of the bailiff, who closed his eyes tightly. Rolling up his sleeves, he dealt a resounding blow to the man's jaw. The bailiff crumpled over in a heap at his feet and lay senseless. Rather disbelieving, Mathis regarded his fist.

'That,' he said, 'is what I should have done to you yesterday, Elias Wasser.'

'Ah,' replied Elias, 'but where would you be now, Mathis?'

They had no trouble locating the path behind the building and from there the northern road. It was mid afternoon and Marta felt relief in leaving the town behind them. After locating the elm trees, they travelled in single file down the path the bailiff had indicated. Elias led, Marta followed, then came Katrina and Mathis and Hans made up the rear. After a trek of an hour or so, they saw the hut, a small stream running close to it.

'Here it is.'

Elias spoke wearily for his back pained him where he had been beaten by Erlin and those burghers who had obeyed him.

'Let us sit down and have a bite to eat before we decide what to do.'

'Decide what to do? Shall we not stay here the night before we travel on? You need to rest. As it is you have travelled too long already. What say you, Katrina?'

Marta turned to speak to her serving woman but she was not there.

'Where is Katrina?'

There was no answer. Hans and Mathis looked sheepish and then Hans spoke.

'She bent to tie the laces in her shoe and bid us continue. She would catch up, she said.'

'And looked you not back?'

'I did,' Mathis avowed.

'Well, and ...'

'Well, and I saw her trailing and turn off into the bushes and I thought well, she must want privacy, you know ...'

'And then?'

Marta's voice grew sharper.

'And then such a bonny bird flew by and I saw a hare and ... and I clean forgot to turn around again until just now.'

Marta sighed and Elias intervened.

'When was it, lads, that this happened?'

Hans and Mathis exchanged glances.

'Oh, about one half hour ago.'

'She will be here shortly then, I think.'

He sat down on the grass in front of the hut and closed his eyes. Marta, after hesitating a moment, followed suit, as did Mathis and Hans. They waited and waited and eventually Mathis and Martin got up and went back to look, but found no trace of Katrina. They supped then while Mathis stood guard some several hundred feet away from the hut watching the path. Elias was uneasy. He questioned Marta closely as to Katrina's loyalty but the girl vowed that Katrina was true, and Hans and Mathis confirmed her words.

'I warrant,' said Marta, 'that she has gone back for some good reason of which,' she added, 'I have no knowledge and that, if we wait, she will be here tomorrow.'

But, although she tried, Marta could not think of what that reason might be and could offer no plausible explanation as to why Katrina had disappeared.

The hut was bare, with not a scrap of furniture in it but a small cot, hard and covered with old straw. Elias, after they had eaten, laid his cloak on it and bade Marta to lie down and sleep. She said she was not sleepy and would sit up awhile.

'If Katrina comes, she will come whether you are asleep or awake,' Elias said, 'there is no point in staying up for her.'

'There is truth in that,' Marta answered, 'so perhaps I shall try to sleep for a while.'

She lay down and although the affairs of the day ran through her mind like a pack of wild dogs, her eyelids grew heavy and closed. Mathis and Hans opted to stay outside under the open stars. It became a clear and starry night.

Towards the morning Marta woke. Elias slept like a sentry near the threshold and she regarded him for a long while. Who was this man and what would this day bring both of them? Later, as they breakfasted on more of the bailiff's bread and drank water from the stream, it was agreed that they should stay another day to wait for Katrina. Bored by the prospect of sitting about, Mathis and Hans walked back down the trail to see if they could catch any wildlife for a meal and also to see if there was any sign of Katrina.

'Are you not worried that the bailiff will send men out after us?'

'No, I think he will not,' Elias responded, 'he was truly afraid of Tetzel and this Erlin who seems to be in his service. I think he will leave well enough alone for fear of being implicated.'

'Do you think Erlin is a true priest?'

Elias grinned before he answered.

'True? No, the man is not true. And that would immediately disqualify him for the priesthood, I think.

'What if Katrina does not return?' Marta continued.

'Well, then I will go and look for her,' Elias reassured.

She digested this information and crumpled a piece of her robe with her fingers.

'What do you do, Elias Wasser, when you are not travelling the roads helping those who need help?'

'I am a student of theology.'

Marta studied Elias' face as he sat across from her on the grass in front of the hut.

'You have not the face of a priest,' she said at length.

'Perhaps that is because I am not going to be a priest.'

'Why then ...?'

She stopped, an unspoken question trailing her words.

'Because I like to learn.'

'Where are you from, Elias Wasser?'

'From Wittenberg, Marta, and that not too long ago.'

'From Wittenberg?'

'Yes.'

'You know that I am from Wittenberg. Why did you not say earlier that you were from the same city?'

'I suppose I did not think it necessary and actually I am not really from Wittenberg, but Northeim, just south of Wittenberg. I have only lived in Wittenberg these last few years as a student.'

'Well, you must come and see my father and myself when you can spare time from your studies. Why,' she continued curiously, 'did you choose to study theology?'

'I had a friend who was a student at the university. He questioned many things, as I did myself and recommended his teacher, a doctor of theology, a man by the name of Luther.'

'I have heard of Luther. That is to say, I have heard nothing but bad about him from our priest, Father Stenck,' Marta said.

'That is because Luther, by his teachings, takes away your Father Stenck's manner of living. Luther tells ordinary people – people like yourself – things they do not know, things they ought to have heard from their priests. Most priests, I trow, have never read the Bible. Have you ever read the Bible, Marta?'

'No ... well, that is, ... Father Stenck does not hold with the laity reading the Bible.'

'Why not?'

'He says it is too difficult and that we shall be confused.'

'You do not make the impression on me as being dull-witted, Marta.'

Marta could see that Elias was laughing at her by the twinkle in his eyes. She stood up and walked a few feet away. With her back towards him, she responded.

'Perhaps I am dull-witted, for I work very hard and seem to get nowhere. I try my best and am not satisfied. I say so many Hail Marys that I sometimes lose count and my Pater Nosters are legion so that they too have almost become meaningless in my heart. I have such a hunger to know what it is that God requires so that I ... so that my mother ...'

She stopped and turned to look at him. Her eyes were filled with tears.

'I know,' Elias replied, 'for I too had that hunger. But I have been fed and I am satisfied.'

'Tell me,' Marta said, and sat down across from him again, 'how it came about.'

'Dr. Luther said and rightly so,' Elias began, 'that the Bible is alive and speaks to you; that it has feet and runs after you; and that it has hands and lays a hold of you. It came about through the Bible, Marta.'

'Do you have a Bible here?' she asked.

'Yes.'

'Can you read some to me? In German, I mean?'

'Yes. I can.'

He said nothing else but took a book from his pack, opened it, searched for a moment and then stopped.

'You may not understand it all, Marta. But that is all right. We can speak of it afterwards.'

She nodded and smoothed her skirt with her hands, eyes on his face.

'This is from Hebrews 7. The good Dr. Luther has just this year begun to lecture on it. I may make a bit of a muddle of it as I translate rather freely. This piece speaks about Jesus as a priest. And this is what it says: 'The former priests were many in number, because they were prevented by death from continuing to be priests ... but He, that is Jesus, is a priest always because He lives forever. So He can save those who draw close to God through Himself, because He always lives to intercede ... to mediate.'

He stopped and looked at her. She nodded again and he continued.

'It is right that we should have Jesus as priest – holy, blameless, without spot, separate from sinners, high in the heavens. Jesus does not have to offer sacrifices every day, like the other priests had to, for his own sins or for those of the people; He only had to offer one time ...'

Elias looked up again at Marta and added, 'I found this part very important for myself,' before he continued, 'Jesus only had to offer a sacrifice one time for all people and that was when He offered up Himself.'

Marta was picking at the grass when he finished the last sentence, and she did not speak. He picked up the Bible and reread the last verse again.

Then, she said softly, 'Mass – my mother and I went to Mass every day.'

'Yes,' he answered, 'I know'

'We were told to go to Mass. The Host is Jesus and we were told that He is being sacrificed again and again. Not just the one time ... The priest, he ... but you say ...'

He flicked through the pages of his Bible until he came upon some verses further on. Then he continued to read, speaking before he did.

'Listen to another text from Hebrews. It reads: Jesus appeared once for all at the end of the age to put away sin by the sacrifice of Himself. And just as it is appointed for men and women to die once, and after that comes judgment, so Jesus, having been offered once to bear the sins of many, will appear a second time, not to deal with sin but to save those who are eagerly waiting for Him.'

Marta stood up again, grass clinging to her skirt. She walked a few feet away and then paced back.

'Shall I ...' said Elias but she interrupted.

'No, don't. I didn't understand all of it. Just a bit of it. I want to think about it. I wish I could talk to my mother about it. We went to Mass together every day,' she repeated again rather dully, 'She is ... she is, dead, you know.'

She looked at the sky and then at him again.

'I wish you had been there before my mother died.'

'We will talk of it more later, I promise you, Marta,' Elias said softly, 'But before I have to give you another letter.'

'No, I do not want to hear another text. I cannot bear so much knowledge in my heart all at once. I do not know where to put it.'

'I do not mean another text.'

'What then?'

'I have a letter written to you by your father. He asked me to give it to you.'

Her face became all wonder.

'How do you happen to know my father?'

It was only after Elias had explained at length, that Marta opened the envelope and began to read the letter contained in it. Excusing himself, Elias left her to privacy and wandered onto the path that seemed to veer north and that, he hoped, would meet up again with the main road. He had no idea what Lazar had written down for his daughter to read. After adding the postscript, he had handed him the envelope and closed his eyes. Elias had tucked the missive away into his pocket and had continued to watch over the ill man.

Marta read the first paragraph several times, hoping she misunderstood its meaning. Then she went on to the second.

... As I write this, I know that I too shall soon be no more ...

Tears coursed down her face and she began to sob.

... Do not reproach yourself for leaving me. Rest assured that I am content to go. I have tried to pray these last days. Yes, your old profligate father who scorned you and your mother's religion – he tried to pray. But not to those stone idols, those lifeless statues to whom you always genuflected. But enough! I would be content if I knew that you were safe. I am putting the deed to our summer home in Salzburg in this envelope. It is in your name. And I buried, this morning, the strong box with the gold in it by our secret spot. I should

not rest easy in my grave if that black-robed raven who calls himself your mother's cousin, should get his hands on your inheritance. And I trust he will try when he finds out I am ill. Never, Marta, never, become a nun as he will most certainly try to persuade you to become should I die! Worry not for my soul, child.! Worry not!

'What do I want with money,' Marta whispered, kissing the page, 'when you, dear ones, are gone? My mother and my father. Forsaken ...'

She wiped her eyes on her skirt and began to read the rest. But just at that moment a noise down the path in front of her caused her to startle. Looking up she saw Hans and Mathis, half-walking, half-carrying Katrina, as she hobbled between them. They settled Katrina on the small cot in the hut. Marta sent Hans to the stream to fetch some water, and she herself knelt by the bed, holding Katrina's bruised hands in her own. Mathis stood in the doorway.

'What happened, dear heart?' Marta said, 'what happened? Where have you been to come back so sore and bleeding? Why did you leave?'

Katrina gazed at her with eyes so sad and filled with such sorrow that Marta wept at seeing them.

'Do not look at me like that,' she said, 'for so mother looked at me before she died and I cannot bear for you to leave me now too.'

'I ...,' whispered Katrina, 'it was I who lost the relics. It was my fault, and for that reason perhaps your dear mother shall have to suffer in purgatory longer than ...'

Marta put a finger on her lips.

'Hush,' she said, 'hush. It is not so.'

'I tried,' Katrina went on, 'I really tried. But it didn't work. I am so sorry.'

Hans came in with some water in his hat and Marta ripped off a piece of her petticoat and dipped it in the liquid. She bathed the welts on Katrina's face and hands and all the time murmured, 'It'll be fine, dear one. Don't worry. I shall take care of you.'

At length, Katrina pushed her away.

'I need to tell you, Marta. I need to tell you why I left.'

Marta left off speaking and sat very quietly, reaching for Katrina's hands again as she began to speak.

'I left yesterday because I thought that I might, by returning to the town by myself, escape detection. I thought that without the others, I might not be noticed. It was not difficult to find my way back and the gate was still open. Besides that, the man of whom you spoke, had just entered the city by the south gate and everyone was agog to see him. I followed the crowd and saw this Tetzel at the head of a procession. He carried a big red cross, and had a stern face, a face I should be afraid of should I meet it on a dark night ...'

She stopped and Marta ran the cloth over her face again.

'Please, might I have a small drink?'

Mathis ran to the stream, poured some water into a small flask, and came back with it. Marta took it from his hand and helped Katrina sit up and drink. She smiled at them all and continued.

'I followed the procession to the church. As we walked there was such noise! Men were beating drums, others waved flags and still others carried candles. The church bells pealed and I could barely think for all the noise. The procession entered the church and after them, the people. Tetzel set up the cross in front of the high altar and next to it he put a large strongbox – larger even than your father has, Marta.'

Marta's face quivered but she made no response. Katrina continued.

'Then Tetzel climbed the pulpit and began to speak. He has such a voice. I vow it is like an arrow which pierces your heart and bowels and fair undoes whatever is inside you.'

She stopped, swallowed, and left off speaking until Hans, impatient with the story asked her what the man Tetzel had said that should cause her to be so afraid.

'It is not that I was afraid,' Katrina said, 'it is more that I was made to shudder. For he had a voice like thunder. 'If the cross that I carried is despised,' he said, 'heaven will rain down fire and brimstone on this city and none of you here shall ever reach paradise. He spoke so loud it was as if his words themselves were fire and brimstone. And everyone was silent. I myself durst not breathe. And then he said that he could sell us indulgences to take away our sins. He said that these indulgences pardoned even sins which people had not committed yet but intended to commit.'

'Well, I might have bought one of those indulgences,' said Hans, 'and then I would have knocked him down flat, taken my money back, and been forgiven at the same time.'

He laughed at that and so did Mathis, but Marta bade both of them be quiet with a severe look.

'You ought not laugh,' Katrina said, 'for it was a serious business. 'Which of you,' Tetzel said, 'has not a sister, a mother, a father, or a brother who even now is burning in purgatory? Who here has the heart to say that he would not pay to have him or her come out?' My hands shook for I did so think of my mistress and of my parents for indeed, they have been dead these many years – and where are they now?'

'Shh,' Marta said, 'do not upset yourself.'

Katrina went on.

'Tetzel said, 'Can you not hear their voices? They cry out to you in their agony.' And indeed, I could hear them. I could hear them weeping and wailing. And I hear it now.'

Closing her eyes, she put her hands over her ears and rocked back and forth as she lay on the cot.

'Shh,' said Marta again, 'shh, my Katrina. We are here and we all love you.'

Katrina opened her eyes.

'It's my fault we lost the relics,' she moaned, 'it's truly my fault.'

'No, it's mine,' Mathis said, 'not yours, you silly woman.'

'Now we have nothing,' Katrina went on in a mournful tone, 'not even a single relic and no indulgence either, because when I went outside later and approached the confessional stalls that had been set up, I went into a booth where Erlin von Reicht happened to be the monk who was giving shrift. Truly I did not know it was him until he spoke out in the booth. He recognized me at once and ordered some of his men to take me to the bailiff. He said I was wicked and likely to cause a disturbance for his worship, Tetzel.'

She stopped and coughed and Marta gave her some more water. Set on finishing the tale, however, she would not stop talking.

'It was a good thing Erlin von Reicht did not oversee the men taking me down to the bailiff, for I pleaded with the men as we were walking. I begged them to let me buy an indulgence before they took me away.

The one fellow, there were two, was rather good-natured and he said to the other, 'Why not. Is it not another coin or two for his Holiness?' So I took out some of the gold coins I had saved in the hem of my skirt. But the other fellow, on seeing the gold, conferred with the first fellow who nodded and left.

The remaining man then grabbed my arm and walked me, not towards the counter where Tetzel stood dispensing indulgences, but towards a secluded alley where I suspected he wanted to take the money from me. He also began to make quite free with me, but I scratched, bit and hit him as hard as I could. I also stuck him with the pin of the clasp which you had bidden me to hide in the folds of my coat. This set him to howling and he let go of me and I ran. I ran as fast as I could through several twists and turns of the alley. I came across a small stairs attached to one of the ramshackle houses in the lane. The stairs had a small gate under it. I was too tired to run much further and I could hear the voices of pursuers behind me. So I opened the gate and almost fell into a dark space full of cobwebs and other things. Pulling the gate shut behind me, I crouched down and began to say Hail Marys.'

'Oh, Katrina!' Marta bent over and kissed Katrina's cheek.

'Mind you,' Katrina said softly, 'I said them in my heart and not out loud. Almost a minute later I could hear footsteps and some men stopped in front of where I was hiding. They spoke and one of them was Erlin von Reicht and, this is the strange part, I could swear that the voice of one of the others belonged to Father Stenck. Perhaps he was because whoever it was seemed to know you, Marta. He berated the men with him for letting me escape and offered a reward should they find me. 'Marta Reiss,' he said, 'must be found at all costs.'

It was quiet. Katrina took another drink of water and continued.

'The men left and why not one of them thought to try the gate behind which I was hidden, I do not know. But I stayed there for a long while. Eventually, I dared open it. The lane was empty and I made, it seems, a good guess as to where the gates were. Everyone was still in the square, buying indulgences. I reached the city gates and ran down the road, but thinking the better of it after a few hundred feet, I jumped into the hedge and lay down thinking that the men might still pursue me. Again I waited and at length fell asleep. When I awoke it was dark and I knew I should not be able to make my way back to you until morning. And here I am.'

Marta kissed Katrina and then stroked her bruised cheek.

'You should not have gone back,' she said.

'I only wanted to give you an indulgence for ... for ...'

She could not continue speaking for now she had reached her tears. Marta held her and hushed her and at length she stopped weeping.

'I must tell you all something,' Marta then said, 'Please Hans and Mathis, come closer, for this is important.'

The men came and stood closer to the cot, both awkwardly holding their caps in their hands, ill at ease with the weeping Katrina had done and edgy because of her story.

'I ...' Marta began, taking her father's crumpled letter from the pocket of her dress, 'I ... must tell you that I have a letter here ... from my father.'

Katrina half-sat up, eyes wide and Hans took a step forward.

'How came you ...?' Katrina began and both men nodded, 'How came you by such a letter?'

'By the hand of Elias.'

They all turned their eyes to the doorway, expecting to see him appear.

'No, he is not here,' Marta said, following their gaze, 'He has gone for a walk to see what might lie beyond this hut.'

'How came he, then,' Katrina went on , 'by such a letter?'

'Well, he ...'

Marta bit her lip. She was close to losing her calm. It had only been Katrina's need of her that had stopped her from flinging herself down on the grass outside and wailing like a child.

'The plague came to Wittenberg while we were gone. Many people died ... '

'Your father?' Mathis called out, his face white, 'Is he ...?'

Marta bowed her head. Tears ran down her cheeks. Katrina was at her side in an instant, arms about the girl.

'Yes, he is dead! My father is dead!' she sobbed, 'And I have no one left!'

'Hush, my baby!' Katrina whispered, patting her shoulder while sheltering her with an embrace, 'are we not all here? Your Katrina and your Mathis and your Hans.'

'But my father is dead!'

Marta's voice had risen to the hysterical and Mathis clenched his fists, not knowing what else to do. A voice from the doorway startled them all.

'Yes, he is, dear child, and it is for that reason that I have travelled the roads and byways to try to find you these last few weeks.'

'Father Stenck.'

Marta managed the words with difficulty. Half-repulsed, half-comforted, she did not know how to interpret his appearance.

'I served him last rites, daughter, and he bade me tell you ...'

He stopped and bent to enter the low doorway of the hut. Mathis and Hans moved as one to the wall and stood silent.

Father Stenck, his bulk overpowering, stepped towards where Marta stood, Katrina's arms still about her.

'He was at ease, daughter. Put your mind at rest about that. And, in the end, was received into the arms of Mother Church.'

Marta still said nothing but stood as stone in Katrina's embrace. She found it almost impossible to think coherently. Father's Stenck's face, a face to which she had often confessed, filled her with memories of her mother.

'He bade me tell you,' the priest continued, 'and was happy that I as a distant kinsman would take the message, that he no longer opposed you seeking the veil. Indeed, it was his wish ... his last wish, I might add, that I escort you to ...'

'Liar!!'

Startled, they all looked beyond Father's Stenck's black robes, and saw Elias standing in the doorway.

'Liar!' he repeated and pointing his index finger at the priest.

Everyone stared at Elias, his face earnest and sincere. Marta looked from him to Father Stenck and her mind was in a turmoil.

'This man, daughter,' the priest said, 'is wanted for theft back in ...'

'No,' she said, 'He is no thief. I know that. But my father ...'

She stopped and looked at Elias helplessly. There was so much pain in her and all she could add was three limp words.

'He is dead.'

'No, Marta! No! I'm sorry that you gained that impression. I do not know what your father wrote in the letter but I do know this: your father was alive and well when I left him.'

'What do you mean? Alive and well? He told me in the letter that he was going to die ...that he had the plague.'

'Indeed,' added Father Stenck, 'and as I said ...'

'Liar!' interrupted Elias, 'Keep your mouth closed or the devil will have you before your time. Your father did have the plague, Marta. I feared he would die. When it seemed death was nigh, I took measures. I had heard that lancing the boils, which he had under his armpits, relieves pressure and lets out the illness. There was no one to help so though I feared I would make a poor doctor, I took a knife and ...'

He did not wish to recount to them the horrible smell and the thick, oozing pus that had flowed from the wounds. For a while he had thought it had been to no avail, but then the old man seemed to fall asleep, breathing in and out, in and out, while he had counted the time between breaths – fearing that each one would be his last. He had prayed for Lazar; he had prayed on his knees at the bedside, beseeching God for his life. And later, when it became apparent that Lazar was really sleeping like a baby, he had thanked God for the man's life, again on his knees by the bedside. And then there had been the matter of a priest suddenly knocking at the door, a priest who wanted very much to know how Herr Reiss was. To get rid of the man he had intimated that Lazar was succumbing to the plague and that it was unhealthy to stay about. The priest had blanched at that and backed up, disappearing almost as quickly as he had come.

'And ...' Marta asked, 'and did the lancing provoke a cure?'

'Yes,' he smiled at her, 'it did indeed. Although the hand of God was in it, to be sure.'

'To be sure,' she murmured, 'to be sure.'

Then she crumpled to the floor and Katrina almost fell down with her.

When Marta came to, she was lying on the small cot and all four, Katrina, Elias, Mathis and Hans were anxiously studying her face. Her first impulse was to laugh for she felt there was a glorious truth in her, but then she recalled vaguely that her father was dead, or perhaps not.

'Father,' she whispered urgently.

'He is alive,' Elias said gently, 'Lazar Reiss, your father is alive.'

'Alive,' she replied and smiled directly at him.

Then sighing deeply, she whispered, 'I would like to hear more, as we travel home.'

O for a heart to praise my God,
A heart from sin set free,
A heart that always feels the blood,
So freely spilt for me.
A heart resigned, submissive, meek,
My Great Redeemer's throne,
Where only Christ is heard to speak,
And Jesus reigns alone.

Charles Wesley

A Heart That Always Feels the Blood

They say it is given to each man to love once in his lifetime. I think that I would agree. And from that one all-encompassing love, they say, flow many other devotions. So, in any case, it was in my life – from one love, many.

My country, France, is a rich country – rich in heritage and in beauty. It is also a wealthy country, able to supply wheat to Spain, Portugal, and England, when we are not at war with them, that is. Our wines are sent to England, Scotland, Flanders, Luxembourg and ... I could go on and on. It is a delicate wine and well worth the crowns its export brings in. We have salt in our country too, salt that preserves – a most precious commodity. It keeps meat and fish better than the German salt which is of an inferior quality. France, as well, has wood for construction and wool for cloth. But I confuse you – first speaking of love and then of my country. But you see, it is all interwoven – artfully interwoven as the fine Camelot cloths made by the skilled weavers in Picardy and Normandy.

My name is Gaspard Palissy. I am the eldest son of Sieur Louis Palissy, a member of the nobility who despised the rich ways of the court. But he was also a man who was, paradoxically, wholly devoted to the royal house. You might call him a 'country gentleman'. He was jolly. He had a great head, a large aquiline nose, full, rounded lips, a bull neck, a broad chest and back, full and wide hips, and slender but quick legs. He was not a tall man and all our acquaintances were unanimous in their agreement that I looked very much like him. My father was almost at all times, as far as I can recall, bright-eyed and cheerful and I can still see him striding around the courtyard of our estate wearing a large felt hat, big boots and a dagger at his belt. Often he would take me with him as he strode with great steps over the land which our Normandy ancestors had bequeathed to us at the cost of many battles. He loved our estate over which he was the unquestioned lord.

My father was married late in life to a girl of Spanish parentage. He had seen her in the entourage of the court. She had somehow captivated him and as she was a ward of the Queen and an orphan with no dowry of which to speak, had not had much trouble in securing permission to wed her. Much younger than he, I remember her mostly for her sweetness. Born of their union in 1535, I recall even now, when I am old and grey, how she sang to me, read to me, and played with me for hours on end, while my father indulgently waved away the normal retinue of wet nurses, servants and tutors that a child usually brings. My mother died when Charles was born, – Charles, my brother, who was seven years younger than I was.

There was a change in my father after my mother's death. Whereas he had always smiled and whistled, he now was often silent, brooding as it were. There were also changes in my life. A tutor, Monsieur de Fail, came to live with us. We were not poor. The farm income and the variety of rents due to my father because of his rank, endowed us with ample sustenance. But money does not make happiness. I would watch my father's silhouette as he walked about the yard. The cheerful swagger had been replaced with a stoop. The bustling figure he had been, content with life and always ready for laughter, was gone. Thus it was I myself, or so I reasoned, that must give affection to Charles. I often held him and the wet nurse would continually have to shoo me out of the nursery. It was no place for growing lads, she said. But I knew better and the shadow of my mother's love guided me.

Charles was as different from my father and myself as night and day. Whereas we were short and stocky, he was slim and lithe. Even in the toddler stage he would stretch his small arms and stand up as tall and as straight as a little sapling and as thin as a willow. Father and I were the oaks. He also showed no interest whatsoever in farm life but was ever curious about books and learning. Monsieur de Fail, even though there was the considerable difference of seven years between Charles and myself, commented dryly that surely the younger son was the brighter. It did not bother me unduly. Indeed, I knew that his words were true. I cared for the land. I knew of which hills our estate was comprised; I was intimately acquainted with the shoulders of our slopes; and I revelled in the joy of breathing fresh air.

My parents were of the Catholic faith. That is to say, my father was a Catholic because he had been born a Catholic. But he was a reflective man who told me that when he compared the treasures of the different churches in France, he thought many were obviously frivolous and fraudulent. He knew that our Lord could not have been crucified with fourteen nails; that an entire length of our courtyard could be hedged with the number of crowns of thorns exhibited; that the number of spears reputed to have pierced Jesus' body was at least four; and that each apostle had multiple bodies. His already weak faith in the Catholic Church was further shaken when on one occasion he found that he had knelt down to a piece of pumice said to be the brain of Saint Peter. Coupled with these obvious discrepancies, there was also the matter of the wealth and power of the clergy. Now if these men had been faithful, honest and caring, that would have affected how we thought about what they taught. But such was not the case. The priests we knew cared little or nothing for the souls entrusted to their care. They only desired the revenues of their benefices. They did not preach; they did not comfort; and they left ordinary folk to the mercy of superstition. Many of them had no Bible learning and had become priests only to avoid the toils of some other occupation.

My brother Charles, even as a child, was very pious. He often went to Mass, fasted and became good friends with the local priest. Brother Borde was, in his own way, actually a likeable sort of fellow. Charles would chide my father and myself for not spending more time in church. We laughed good-naturedly, saying that he was spending enough time there for all three of us. Charles would laugh too and this is how things were in the fall of 1558 when I was twenty and five years old and Charles a young pup of eighteen.

It was a cold, impertinent fall and the rain was icy and constant. The principal outlook of our house was on the east for the early morning sun is from the east and is warming. Besides this, it is well-known that the more easterly a house faces, the less it suffers from storm in the winter. But I digress again. In the late September of that fall, I awoke in the very early hours one morning to hear the sound of a door opening and closing in the wind. My room, which I shared with Charles, was just over the storeroom and cellar. Supposing that someone had left the cellar door unlatched, I rose out of bed and went out to see what I could find. It was a windy but clear night and the stars were magnificent. I stood for a moment, after I had closed the culprit door. By chance, my eye fell on another door, the field door at the side of the paddock. It is a door we have for entering the house when we do not wish to go through the stables and when we do not want others to see us. This door, with faint light shining from it, was half-open whereas it was supposed to be, at all times, shut securely.

I was not afraid, for all men in the area were our friends and we rarely had trouble. It was almost time for the rooster to crow and I imagined that perhaps one of the serving men, having drunk too deeply of cider, had let himself in by the paddock to sleep things off. I walked over to the door and to my surprise heard my father's voice as I came closer. Curious, I opened the door further and came upon him in deep conversation with a middle-aged man. My father saw me before the man did and he motioned that I should enter.

'This is Jerome,' he said rather unceremoniously, 'a pedlar from Geneva.'

'Pedlar?' I answered, mystified, for such men generally arrive in the day time and then do not use the field door.

'Yes,' said my father again, rather emphatically, 'a pedlar.'

I studied the so-called pedlar. He wore a grey cloak and carried a big satchel such as pedlars are wont to carry. His eyes, which he focused squarely on my own, were rather disconcerting. They made me want to look away and yet I could not.

'He peddles somewhat,' my father went on, 'which we have all the time in the world to study before we buy. Is that not so, Jerome?'

Jerome turned back to my father and smiled.

'Yes, Louis,' he replied, 'that is so.'

I thought it passing strange that a pedlar whom I had never seen before, would make so free as to call my father by his Christian name, but said nothing.

'Jerome will stay with us through October. We need extra help to harvest grapes, knock down the walnuts, mow the late meadows and collect straw for the roof of the stables.'

I knew all these things had to be done and did not understand why my father would enumerate them to me.

'Tell your brother when he wakes, and pass on Jerome's arrival to Jacques.'

Jacques was our steward and he slept in the room next to ours.

In the next few days, Jerome made himself useful. I certainly could not fault the man for laziness. He was a good worker. He was also cheerful, singing much as we worked in the fields. It was not until a week after his arrival that my father asked Jerome to show us his merchandise. We were in the kitchen and eating our evening meal. Although not abundant, neither was our table sparse. Serving dishes were set in the middle of the table and there were trenchers – stale bread cut up into large rectangles to serve as plates. The common goblet was kept on a sideboard and wiped with a napkin between uses. I shared a soup bowl with Jerome and was struck at that time by the softness of his hands. Not a pedlar's hands, I thought. And then my father asked him to show his wares. Charles and Monsieur de Fail looked up from their food and Jacques, as well as Pierre and Paul, our hired men, stopped working. The four serving girls began to whisper, hoping, no doubt, for trinkets and ribbons and other such things as pedlars usually carry. Jerome stood up and left the kitchen, returning but a minute or so later with his bag. He stood for a moment in the centre of the kitchen, in front of the table where we all sat. Then he reached into his bag and took out a book. It was very quiet although Lucie, one of the younger serving girls, sighed, for she supposed books to be boring and altogether too difficult for herself.

'I have come,' Jerome said, as he held the book in his hands, 'at the express wish of Louis Palissy,' and here he nodded courteously to my father who nodded back, 'to tell you of the Gospel of Jesus Christ, my Lord and Saviour.'

Pierre, who was a most profane man but who worked like an ox, swore under his breath. But a glance from my father made him look down at the ground. Charles seemed very discomfited and fidgeted.

'My name is Jerome, as you all know,' Jerome smiled as he continued to speak, 'Jerome Seguin. The last few years I spent in Switzerland where I studied with the preacher Theodore Beza. There were many men there besides myself – many men from France. A number of them, myself included, decided to return to France to share what we learned with people like yourself.'

'You are under the Pope's curse.'

It was Charles who spoke and I was astonished to hear fire in the words of my otherwise so agreeable, albeit impetuous, brother.

'Yes, I am,' Jerome was not at all flustered as he answered, 'but I have God's blessing and, with your father's blessing as well, I will speak to you of things you have perhaps never heard before. Please feel free to stop me and ask questions, if you want.'

'The Edict of Chateaubriand, which the King felt fit to pass seven years ago, forbids the bringing into France of any books from Geneva and other places rebellious to the Church.'

This time it was Monsieur de Fail who spoke and Charles nodded eagerly, even as he turned his trencher around with his finger.

'Ah,' Jerome said slowly, 'but, as I will explain to you this evening, we must obey God rather than man where man's law conflicts with His most holy Word.'

He held up the Bible for all to see. It was the first time I had seen a Bible. We, all of us strained our eyes. Father asked if he might hold it and Jerome passed it around the table. We fingered the leather cover, opened it up and stroked it. But holding words is like holding food in one's fingers; one must taste before there is satisfaction.

Jerome spoke to us all evening. Light was provided by the tallow candles. There was also the light from the fire in the hearth. After the initial distrust had worn off, there was an ease in our kitchen. Jerome spoke well and he spoke convincingly. We had all worked with him for several days and liked the man. As I said before, he was not lazy and lent his hands to whatever was put before him. I went to bed that evening thinking that I was closer now to being a believer than being an atheist. From the time I had grown out of short pants, you see, and had been entrusted with hard chores, I had always fancied myself an atheist, although I must be quick to add that the beauty of nature had always awoken in me a profound desire to praise a creator.

'What thought you, Gaspard?' Charles whispered from his bed.

'I thought he was well-spoken,' I whispered back, 'almost as well-spoken as my brother.'

He threw something at me in the dark and laughed softly from his corner of the room.

'I think that I will become of the new religion, Gaspard.'

'Isn't that a rather quick decision?' I answered sleepily, already half-gone.

'No,' Charles' retort was quick in coming, 'I know that I believe what he says and I want to learn more.'

My young brother became Jerome's shadow that winter, for you see, Jerome's stay extended beyond what my father had originally said. He was at the man's side as we made wine in October and as we collected acorns in November. And, as the snow fell in December, Charles constantly engaged him in debates at the fireside. Monsieur de Fail was not far behind and seemed just as eager to learn. In the spring of the following year, we began to have meetings with some of our neighbours. Father rigged up a platform of sorts in one of the barns and invited people to come at set times to hear Jerome preach. It was at one of these meetings that I first met Madeleine Sicort. She was the daughter of one of the neighbouring landowners. Monsieur Sicort, like father, farmed at leisure and administered his lands with fairness and joy. She was beautiful, Madeleine, and when she first came I could not listen to Jerome but could only stare at her face. It was the same with Charles, who, as usual, could not keep his wild thoughts to himself.

'I want to ask father if he will approach Monsieur Sicort for her hand.'

'You have only just met the girl a few times.'

'Yes, but I know ...'

'What if she does not like you?'

'Why should she not like me?'

Indeed, why should she not like Charles? He was young, good-looking, and the fact that he was the younger son should not deter her, for father had always told us he would divide the inheritance equally between us. I loved Charles and if Madeleine and he were to marry, I would be happy for them. Besides, with my bull-neck and stocky body, she was not overly likely to take any interest in me, a fellow who knew more about lambings, fox trappings, autumn fever, and cleaning out ditches, than how to speak in theological or flowery, romantic terms.

If we were just a trifle hidden away in our farming community in Normandy, we were not unaware of the fact that all of France blazed with the funeral pyres of those of the new religion. It did not worry us unduly, for we reckoned that sooner or later French society would have to recognize that those of the Reformed persuasion were loyal French citizens; we were certain that laws would be enacted which would give freedom of religion to all. Rumour had it that there was no town, province, or trade which did not have adherents to this new Truth. But can truth be new? As for me, I was uncertain as to what my heart embraced.

Father took all things in his stride. It was a fact that since Jerome had come, he was more talkative and content. It was in April, around St. George's Day, that he spoke to me of his feelings for the new religion. We had been digging around the feet of the orange and lemon trees, taking out the surface roots and the excess branches, not allowing even one branch to cross another. It was tedious work but good work, this pruning. From there we moved onto the grafting.

'I feel, Gaspard,' my father said, 'that I have been grafted.'

It was not like my father to speak thus in lofty language. He was a realistic man who never related dreams or thoughts beyond what he could see. But I understood what he said. He had accepted the new religion. He went on.

'I have a friend in Paris. I want you to take Charles there. He is a good man, Annas du Bourg, a nephew of the late Chancellor of France and a learned man, a defender of liberty.'

He paused for breath after such a long sentence and then went on.

'Our Charles will, no doubt, benefit greatly from being in his household for a time. Monsieur de Fail has taught Charles much, but the boy's knowledge is at a standstill right now. Besides that, he is much too young to think of marriage.'

I smiled behind my tree and thought that Charles, in his exuberant puppy love, had probably spoken impetuously to father about his feelings for Madeleine.

'When do you want me to take Charles?'

'At the end of May, after the sheep shearing.'

We were received most courteously by Master Annas du Bourg, Counsellor to the King of France. I stayed for two weeks, as my father had instructed and then returned to our estate in Normandy, leaving Charles in the safe care of Master du Bourg, a jurist and one of the most learned men I have ever met. No doubt, Charles would receive much in the way of education from him.

It was at the end of July, just as we were harvesting the wheat and the vegetables that Charles returned home. He was not expected, as my father had strictly enjoined upon him that he was to stay with Master du Bourg at least until Martinmas. He was very distraught and almost fell into our arms off the horse he was riding. My initial instincts were to hold him, as I had done when he was but a toddler and he had fallen and hurt himself. Charles' first words, given through heavy breathing, were that we must raise an army, that we must call together all Reformed men and storm the Bastille. My father calmly handed Charles' lathered horse over to Pierre. Then he led Charles away from the gawking servant girls. I followed shortly afterwards, first giving instructions that everyone should continue with their work.

Father's private quarters were on the east side of the house. They overlooked the garden and enabled him to see the men and to know who came and went. Charles was drinking some wine and father had seated himself opposite my brother when I opened the door. I stood on the threshold, but father motioned for me to come in and to shut the door behind me.

'Now tell me slowly,' father began, looking at Charles, 'what happened and what made you return home so quickly.'

Charles took a deep breath. He looked haggard and pale and his hands, as they put down the goblet, shook.

'Kind Henri, as you know, called a Mercuriale – a meeting of the judges and rulers of senate.'

We had not known, but we nodded, my father and I. Charles continued, his voice growing stronger as he went on.

'Master du Bourg, as jurist, was obliged to go and asked me to accompany him as his secretary. I was to take down notes and to learn from the general assembly of good French men, he said, as they met together to see to matters of the administration of the kingdom.'

We nodded again but Charles seemed not to note us now and spoke as if to himself.

'Because the hall at the palace, where Parliament usually meets, was being prepared for the marriage of the Princess Elizabeth, the Mercuriale met at the monastery of the Augustinian friars by the Seine River. What men I saw there – lawyers, nobles, and even the Princes of the Blood, Antoine de Bourbon, Duke of Vendôme, and his brother, Louis de Bourbon, Prince of Condé. Now although the object of a Mercuriale is law and order, the royal Procureur-General, Monsieur Bourdin, announced that all had been called together to find out whether their sentiments lay for or against the new religion and that they would be asked to vote accordingly. My heart beat in my throat as he announced this. I did not fear for myself, for who cared where my sentiments lay? But I feared for Master du Bourg.'

He stopped and took another drink of wine. My father shifted in his chair and began to look anxious.

'There has always been, as Monsieur de Fail taught me,' Charles went on, 'free declaration of sentiment in which members are allowed to hold views divergent from those of the crown. And I think that most members were ready to vote for their own views until, wholly unexpectedly, his Majesty, the King, walked into the meeting. He came in state, accompanied by his noblemen and by the archers of his bodyguard. He sat upon a throne made ready for him and then proceeded to address everyone there.'

Charles was quiet now and sombrely stared out the window.

'What said the king?' my father demanded to know.

Charles looked at him. There were tears in his eyes.

'He said that the true religion of France was that of Rome and that his daughter Elizabeth would be wed to Philip of Spain, that monster of the Inquisition ...'

'Surely he did not use those words,' my father interrupted.

Charles smiled a thin smile.

'No, those were my own words. The King went on to say that he would devote his reign to reestablish the true faith and that he hoped his counsellors would share his opinion.'

I wondered what I should have done, had I been placed in such a position as the counsellors. But it was not likely that I would ever be in such a position. Not I who even now was thinking of manuring vines and rooting out dog-tooth.

'How did du Bourg react?'

'Oh, father, how can you who have called him a friend for so many years, ask? Du Bourg made no attempt to hide his faith in the new religion and spoke most eloquently. He said that many crimes and wicked actions, such as oaths, adulteries and perjuries, went without correction. He also pointed out that at the same time tortures were applied each day to men whose only crime seemed to be that they prayed for the King, obeyed the law, and defended order. He justly went on to say, even as he looked straight at the King, that it was a grave matter to condemn to the flames those who died calling on the name of the Lord Jesus.'

There was a hush in our father's room after Charles spoke these last words. It seemed to me that the lark bursting forth into sweet song just outside the window did not sing as purely as du Bourg's words had been.

'What happened?'

My father asked softly and Charles, after briefly studying his hands, continued.

'The votes were read by the King who, with the papers in his hand, became red in the face. He then stood up and said that he was extremely displeased to find that many of his counsellors had left the faith. After this he ordered two of the counsellors, Louis de Faur and Annas de Bourg, arrested by the Constable of France. The Constable, in turn, called upon Count Montgomery, Captain of the Scottish bodyguard. The Captain took Louis de Faur and Annas de Bourg to the Bastille. Three other judges were arrested a short while later as well and many others left Paris in haste to escape similar fates.'

'And how fares he, my friend, Annas de Bourg?'

'He has been shut up in an iron cage.'

Jerome was, at this time, still with us. That is to say, he travelled back and forth across France, and then came back home to roost with us, as it were. The number of believers in our area had grown, and even the local priest, Brother Borde, faithfully attended the sermons. Madeleine and her father continued to come as well. Charles took to walking out with Madeleine on those days that we had preaching. They would wander together, the two of them, in the woods, their heads close together as they talked. I tried not to envy Charles and was glad that, should he eventually marry her, I would at least be able to call Madeleine my own dear sister.

Only some two weeks later, as we were sorting out the apples and pears, and picking those off the trees which weighed them down, a messenger arrived for father. Sweaty and tired from a hard ride, the man stood in front of father in our orchard. He wore du Bourg's livery and spoke haltingly.

'The King is dead.'

We all stopped working and edged closer. My father did not stop us. The pungent smell of ripe fruit permeated the air and laced the story the rider then proceeded to tell us.

'Splendid preparations had been made for the Princess Elizabeth's wedding. There were marvellous decorations, tables of food and ... and ...'

Talking pell-mell, the fellow stopped a moment for air. Father motioned that he should take it easy and the man resumed at a slower pace.

'... much entertainment had been arranged. Lists were erected in the wide street of St. Antoine. The windows on either side were occupied by the nobility so that they could see France's best knights perform great feats of skill.'

I thought of Pierre and Paul as they dug up the ground for a well; I could see father make his honey and beeswax; and I could envision the servant girls bend over the artichokes, covering them so that the frost could not get into them. Surely those were feats of skill far greater than some men riding horses and poking lances at one another. Unfortunately, I had lost some of the man's tale by my reflections.

'... also a stake, piled high with wood, at the feast. It was reserved for five prisoners, hidden away in the dungeons of the Bastille ...'

Here Charles groaned and the man, distracted by the sound, stopped for a moment before he kept going. It was now evident that he was beginning to enjoy the riveted attention of the group and he increased in volume.

'The tourney began. I doubt that you can picture it.'

He looked at us as one looks at country bumpkins, and I wondered if he had ever pollarded trees with excess branches or grafted olives which needed budding.

'The notes of the hautboy and the clarion sounded high and clear. The King pursued pleasure and at the same time courted pain. The moment the tourney was over it was reported that Montgomery, the Captain of the Guard, would bring out the five men, put out their eyes with the sword and then torture them before burning them at that stake.'

We all shuddered involuntarily. How horrible it seemed! And how far away from the grove where we were presently standing. The bees companionably buzzed about us, and the fragrance of mown meadows and ripe fruit encompassed us like a comfortable tunic.

'At the close of the festivities the King himself wanted to enter the lists and break a lance in honour of Diana of Poitiers, she who was his mistress and not his wife. He chose as antagonist Montgomery, the Captain of the Guard. They rode against one another and Montgomery's lance hit the King's visor. It was not clear to anyone whether the King's visor was not clasped on properly or whether it simply broke. The sum of the matter is that the lance itself was splintered by the blow and that the piece which Montgomery did not instantly lower, entered the King's eye and penetrated to his brain.'

We all drew in our breath. The messenger continued.

'And so it was that Henri II, King of France, fell off his horse. He was quickly stripped of his armour and taken to a nearby palace. It is said, that as he was carried off the tilting ground he turned his bleeding face towards the prison where the condemned men were waiting to be executed and that he spoke. But no one was clear about this. What we do know is that in the Palais des Tournelles, on July 10th, he died in great pain. Monsieur Gaudet, the steward, commanded me to ride to tell you. Because your son, Monsieur Charles, was in our household for a time, he deemed that you now might want to petition, with others, for Master du Bourg's release.'

It was quite a while before my father spoke.

'Is the King's body lying in state?'

'Yes,' the man answered, happy to have more to contribute, 'and the bed upon which he was laid was covered with a rich piece of tapestry on which is represented the conversion of Saint Paul. The words 'Saul, Saul, why persecutest thou me!' are embroidered on it in large letters.'

A lark sang in the distance, but we were all quiet, impressed with the inscrutable ways of God.

There were petitions. My father easily lent his name, together with others, to a request asking that du Bourg, as well as the other counsellors, be released. Charles slept and ate badly. He could not be induced to work on the farm and my father was at a loss as to what to do with the boy. In the fall we heard that there was to be no reprieve for the counsellors. Indeed, the new King, sixteen-year-old Francis II, was stepping up the persecution of the new religion. But we were hidden in Normandy and continued to hear Jerome preach.

In December, after the wine had been put into the cellar and the acorns collected for pig feed, Charles asked permission to return to Paris. Father was not anxious to let him go. There were so many reports of looting, of treachery and lying against the Reformed, that he felt that Charles would not be safe. I offered to go with him, even though my heart was not in it. Deep within myself I still had not committed to the new faith. On the one hand, there was a guilt within me, a knowledge that every man should stand up for something, and a desire for a creed. On the other hand, I loved my farming and I desired to live in peace. Indeed, I desired to live.

My father hesitantly let us go. It was mid-December but it had been a mild December. The roads were passable and we left in good spirits and well-provisioned. We arrived in Paris at the large estate of du Bourg and were heartily welcomed by his steward, Monsieur Gaudet. But the news he told us of du Bourg was disheartening. The order of his execution had just been given. It was to be at the Place de Grève.

'Master du Bourg is very courageous,' Monsieur Gaudet said, 'and the prison walls resound with the psalms and hymns which he sings to the accompaniment of a lute.'

'He is no longer in a cage?' I asked.

Monsieur Gaudet shook his head.

'At the beginning,' he answered, 'he was shut up in a cage. And passers-by were forbidden to look up at the walls of the Bastille. But later he was released from the cage and shut up in a cell. The lute, an instrument at which he excels, was permitted him.'

I had nothing to reply. It was inconceivable to me that, facing death, one should sing. It made me quiet. Charles, on the other hand, was livid with anger. He pounded the table, hit the wall and thought of a million and one things which he might do in order to rescue Master du Bourg. But there was nothing he could do and we were but two faces in a crowd that late December day when du Bourg was led to the Place de Grève.

So many people came to witness du Bourg's death that a strong guard was set about him. Perhaps the Cardinal of Lorraine was afraid that at the last moment some plot would be hatched to release him. But the people held their peace as du Bourg was marched to his earthly end.

I remember Master du Bourg as a pleasant, sharp-witted man – as a gentleman as well as a gentle man. He had taken in my brother at a moment's notice, glad of an opportunity to pass on knowledge to a country lad. And he was permitted to speak before he died – permitted to pass on knowledge to another country lad – myself. I was glad of it and yet I was not glad. For with many fierce pricks did his words hit my soul and ever afterward I was not the same.

'My friends,' du Bourg cried, and cry he must for thousands were assembled, 'I am here not as a thief or a robber, but for the Gospel.'

Charles was sobbing. I put my arm about him as best I could with the crowd pressing heavy around us.

'No one,' du Bourg went on, 'will be able to separate us from Christ, whatever snares are laid for us, whatever ills our bodies may endure.'

What his body would soon endure I could not bear to think about. I tightened my grip on Charles.

'We know that we have long been like lambs led to the slaughter. Let them, therefore, slay us, let them break us in pieces. For all that, the Lord's dead will not cease to live, and we shall rise in a common resurrection. I am a Christian! Yes, I am a Christian!'

Tears ran down my face and something melted in my heart. I felt a warmth in me such as I had never felt, not even when my mother had embraced me and held me close.

'I will cry yet louder when I die,' du Bourg cried, his countenance assured and his words clear, 'because I die for the glory of my Lord, Jesus Christ. And since it is so, why do I tarry? Lay hands upon me, executioner, and lead me to the gallows.'

All around me it was quiet. No one harangued the prisoner; no one threw rocks or rotten fruit; and there was an air of expectation. Du Bourg turned to his executioners.

'Put an end,' he now said, 'to your burnings, and return to the Lord with amendment of life, that your sins may be wiped away. Let the wicked forsake his way, and the unrighteous man his thoughts, and let him return unto the Lord and He will have mercy upon him. Live, then, and meditate upon this, O senators; and I go to die!'

He was offered a crucifix, large and shining, but he turned his face away. I saw a quiver pass over his features as the executioner approached with a rope to strangle him before his body would be burned.

'My God, forsake me not, that I may not forsake Thee!'

And so du Bourg died but I kept thinking of the seed, the dead seed which I planted every year and which every year sprouted up to bear fruit.

We travelled back to Normandy the next day. Father was very happy to see us alive. We sat by the fireside in those weeks that followed and fashioned endless implements for the household – ladles, tubs, bowls and rakes. Even Charles, for all his learning, sat and whittled. There was strange comfort thus, to sit and watch the flames and warm our chilled bones, all the while remembering those other flames and the words that had been spoken there. Jerome had left us for a few months but had promised to return in the spring. The Sicorts visited but even the beautiful and sweet Madeleine did not give Charles back his usual spirits. Nor myself, I might add. I wished that Jerome was present so that I could speak to him, ask him, confess to him, if need be. But he was gone.

January passed slowly. Father and I, as well as Pierre, Paul and Jacques, worked the land which had not been worked in October. As well, we cut wood and trimmed trees and vines. It was good hard work and I revelled in it. It took thinking away and that is what I needed. Then, early in February, as I was cleaning out our dovecote, Jerome returned. He returned not by himself but with a stranger. I liked not the demeanour of the man who looked to be about forty. He was a bit too bold, too aggressive, for my taste. Introduced as Jean Danton, Jerome told us he had met the man on the road and that he was looking for work. I could see that father was not impressed with Jean either but, out of Christian pity, offered him hospitality and some work. Jean seemed greatly taken by Charles seeking him out for conversation. After a day or so, Charles urged father to keep the man on because he was of the new faith and in danger of being arrested should he return to Paris from whence he hailed. Father shrugged and said that as long as Jean worked hard, he was welcome to stay.

In the after hours, when the sun was low in the sky, Jean could often be seen talking to Charles. They would either disappear for hours on end in the nearby woods, or sit talking in one of the barns. I liked it not and spoke to Charles one evening.

'Jean is taken with you, is he not?' I probed, 'He must have a lot of tales to tell.'

'He's a good man,' Charles replied.

'But who is he?'

'A loyal fellow. One who does not forget du Bourg and one who sees the great need for France to be delivered from the Papist rule of Francis II and his evil counsellors.'

'And how would he go about that?' I asked, curious in spite of myself, 'Raise an army?'

I was joking, of course, but in the darkness of the night Charles jumped out of bed and was at my side in an instant.

'Who revealed this to you?'

I sat up, suddenly aware that things were going on which could be dangerous.

'I was not serious, Charles.'

Even though it was a dark and cool night, I could sense that my brother was sweating freely.

'What are you involved in, brother?'

'Nothing.'

The answer was given dully and I did not think he would easily tell me more.

'Please tell me, Charles. I may be able to help.'

'You won't tell father?'

Even though I was surprised that he might speak freely, I would not give him my word on that.

'That depends.'

'You must give me your word, Gaspard. It is vital that no one should know what Jean has told me.'

'What has he told you then?'

'No, no! You must first give me your word that you will not tell father.'

I capitulated.

'All right then. You have it.'

He grasped my hand and kissed it.

'Thank you, Gaspard. For I do so want to share this with you.'

'Well, what is it then?'

And Charles began to speak.

'There is a man. His name is Godefroy de la Renaudie – a gentleman of ancient family in Périgord. His brother was murdered by the Papists. He travels over a great part of France. He visits the most prominent enemies of the King's uncles, the wicked Guises who rule through the young Francis II, and urges all to unite against them.'

'What does he mean, 'unite against them'?'

'He means assemble together – stand together against the evil regime which we live under. He means stand together as an army until a fair government has been assembled under one of the Princes of the Blood, either Antoine the Bourbon or the Prince of Condé. Both of them, as you know, are said to be of the new religion.'

'And whom would your army fight?'

'It's not my army, Gaspard. It is the army of every law-respecting citizen of France.'

I could hear this fellow Jean talking through my brother. But I have to say as well that part of me exulted in his words. There was nothing I would like so much as to tear down the laws which made people like Madeleine, and others like her, worship in secret.

'If you know that an army is being raised, Charles, it is very likely that most of France is aware of the fact, including the Guise brothers.'

'Oh, no, Gaspard. Everyone who is told about the army is sworn to secrecy, even as I just swore you to secrecy.'

'Does Jerome know?'

'I do not know.'

'May I tell him?'

'I should have to ask Jean.'

'But surely Jean is not in charge?'

'No, he is only recruiting people for Renaudie.'

In the end, Charles gave me permission to tell Jerome. But it turned out that Jerome was already aware of the plot, or conspiracy, as it came to be known. As well, my father knew, and Jacques, Pierre and Paul, and so, it seemed, the whole countryside. So much for Charles' secrecy. Hotly debated at every evening meal, we were not all in agreement with one another.

'The young King Francis, who is even younger than I am, has put the rule of the state entirely into the hands of his wife's uncles.'

Charles talked scornfully, with his mouth full of bread, and addressed Jerome. Jerome looked at my brother kindly before he responded.

'That is so.'

He put down his spoon before he went on.

'But don't forget, Charles, that God in heaven is in control.'

Charles spluttered somewhat, unable to answer quickly. But Jean took over where Charles had left off.

'God has told us in His most holy Word, not to obey that which conflicts with His authority. You tell us that yourself quite often. The Cardinal of Lorraine, that man who has so infamously killed our beloved Master du Bourg, pillages the houses of the faithful in Paris. Everywhere I looked, when I was there but a few weeks ago, I saw armed men on foot and on horseback. And do you know what they were doing? They were leading men, women and children off to prison.'

Pierre swore under his breath but a stern look from Jerome made him blush. Jean went on.

'Street corners are filled with plunder from the houses of those of the new faith. This plunder is offered up for sale. There are countless numbers of children wandering about the streets. They are hungry and have no shelter and there are precious few who dare to offer food to them. Because if people are seen doing so, they themselves stand in danger of arrest.'

It was silent around our dinner table. Father looked thoughtful. He then spoke slowly and ponderously, as if he weighed every word.

'But surely an uprising, such as is proposed by Monsieur Renaudie, cannot succeed. We have not the manpower – nor,' he added after a moment's declaration, 'the leadership that is required.'

'But we do,' Jean said eagerly, 'Indeed, we do.'

'How say you so?' father rejoined dubiously.

'Prior to my coming here, many noblemen met in the city of Nantes, so many as to represent the entire country of France. Four hundred of these nobles were mounted on horse and some two hundred foot soldiers were there as well. Together they planned a resolute course of action. Led by Renaudie they will take the young King Francis, who is only sixteen after all, into custody so that his uncles cannot poison his mind any longer. Once these nobles establish a legitimate government with proper guardians, they will release Francis who will be put back on the throne, under these guardians.'

Father nodded, trying to absorb all the information he had been given. I myself had many thoughts also but did not know where to begin voicing them.

'I am with them.'

Charles spoke boisterously and Paul, who sat next to him, clapped him on the shoulder.

'I also,' he said, but I felt sure Paul was not quite aware of all the intricacies involved and did not understand what he was saying.

'What does this conspiracy involve for us?' I asked.

Jean, scraping back his chair over the rushes, stood up.

'It involves being willing to march on the stronghold of the Guises; taking the young king captive. And encouraging him to rule justly under good counsellors.'

'Even if those of our faith,' Jerome said, 'are victorious, they stand to lose. For if we become a military and political party, we have lost our ...'

Jean did not let him finish but interrupted rather rudely.

'You are not in the majority, Brother Seguin,' he said, 'because most of the French pastors approve of this project, provided a Prince of the Blood comes forward to take leadership.'

'No Prince has,' Jerome rejoined.

The conversation was stopped at this point by father because it was late and, no doubt, he had the next day's work in mind. The weather was excellent and the planting season lay ahead of us.

It was not until a few days later that I understood from Charles that he, as well as Pierre, would be leaving to join others who were beginning to march on the Castle of Amboise. The tenth of March had been chosen as the date to carry out their plan. King Francis had been taken to Blois by his uncles who, it was said, knew of the plot.

'You march to your death then,' I said, greatly discomfited that such a foolish conspiracy would be put into effect.

'Jean says that if an unarmed deputation can get permission to see the King at Blois, all will be well. This deputation will present two requests before his Majesty. The first is that the Guise brothers be dismissed and the second is that liberty of worship be given to all living in France. Surely ...'

'And then, I suppose, you will kidnap him. Charles, even you with all your zeal and optimism must see that this plan cannot succeed.'

I interrupted him rather rudely and he looked at me as if I were a coward. And so he intimated in his next words.

'Even Madeleine goes along.'

'Madeleine?'

I repeated her name foolishly, as one who does not know what he is saying.

'Yes, she has decided that she would like to take part in this demonstration of faith.'

'Demonstration of faith?! Charles, it is rather a demonstration of stupidity! How can you let her do this? What have you been saying to her? How can you encourage ...'

But my brother had disappeared and I saw him a moment later running across the courtyard, meeting up with Jean and making for the woods.

I stayed in our room to think. Most of the time, what with the heavy work outside, I was too tired to formulate thoughts. Now I must take the time. There was that in me which hoped this conspiracy of Renaudie would work. Imagine having the freedom to worship as you liked! No more stories about odious tortures against brave men and women who only sought to worship God. Then my thoughts turned to Madeleine. Who would protect her in the woods surrounding Amboise during the time that Guise soldiers would be swarming around the castle looking for dissidents? I knelt down in front of my bed.

'Oh, God,' I prayed out loud, 'Oh, God, help me!'

The words of du Bourg swam around in my mind and I paddled behind them.

'Let them slay us!' he had said, 'Let them break us in pieces; for all that the Lord's dead will not cease to live, and we shall rise in a common resurrection. I am a Christian! Yes, I am a Christian!'

Compelled beyond reason, I whispered those words, down on my knees, in front of the bed.

'Yes, I am a Christian!'

The same warmth that had encompassed me when I had witnessed du Bourg's execution, now took hold of me again. And I was aware that I truly believed and it was a great joy to me; and yet I still did not know whether or not I should put my weight with the conspirators. But Madeleine's face, serious and reflective, won out over against my objections and I felt I must go along with Charles in order to protect both of them.

I did not receive my father's blessing to leave when I told him of my decision. Or perhaps within himself he did give it, but rebelled against the knowledge that there was a good chance he would see neither of his sons again. Neither did Jerome offer encouragement. But he did say that he understood why I was going. Whether he really did, I do not know.

The Castle of Amboise stood upon a high rocky escarpment. In front of it ran the mighty Loire River. Renaudie had established himself within six leagues of the castle at the beginning of March, and made arrangement for his plans to be carried out within the next two weeks. We arrived during this time and found lodging at a nearby inn. But we also sought out those encamped in the woods and together with many others sat around campfires in the evening and discussed the possibilities of success. The plan was that Renaudie was to send his troops into the town of Amboise in small detachments, so as not to attract attention. He himself was to enter on some date around the middle of March. During the days and nights we spent there I missed the farm, the planting and the feel of the soil. I hated the uncertainty of our situation as we waited and waited, biding our time until Renaudie was ready. Renaudie's soldiers, we were told, would seize the castle gates and arrest the Guise brothers. It sounded so simple, so unspeakably easy, as hopefuls reiterated the plan again and again into the flames of the campfires. After the arrest, a signal would be displayed on top of the tower and men-at-arms, hidden in the woods around us, would rush in and complete the take-over of the castle.

Unfortunately, there was a traitor. This really came as no surprise to me because a secret distributed over so large a contingent as thousands of people is bound to leak. The Guises consequently changed the King's guard, built up the gate of the city wall and dispatched troops into the surrounding towns. Renaudie didn't stand a chance. As his soldiers were advancing on Amboise, he was killed in an ambush. His men were either hacked into pieces or taken prisoners. We, in the relative safety of the inn during that particular day, were not aware of the intense dangers surrounding us. But we found out quickly enough when a messenger arrived covered with blood. He had been with a company of soldiers to the left of Renaudie, and had been shot in the shoulder. The inn-keeper bound up his wound and advised us to hide. The man with the bullet wound nodded in agreement.

'Yes,' he said, 'you young people will do well to leave here immediately.'

Madeleine was very brave throughout all this. Her calm demeanour, her steadfastness, her bright smile, all added to my conviction that I had acted rightly in accompanying her and my brother.

'It is best we return home,' I ventured, 'as the cause appears to be lost.'

Charles shook his head.

'It is only this man's word.'

No sooner had he said this than another soldier ran into the inn.

'All is lost,' he called, 'and the Guises vow revenge. They are already building scaffolds in Amboise and an executioner is sharpening his axe in the market-place.'

I put my arm about Madeleine.

'We are going home.'

My voice was firm this time but Charles pushed me aside.

'Coward!' he said, 'To give up so easily.'

'Easily!' I replied, angered by his total disregard for Madeleine, 'What would you have us do? Walk into Amboise and ask the hangman to put a noose about our necks?'

Charles then put the question to Madeleine.

'What are you going to do? Leave with Gaspard or come with me?'

'Where would you go, Charles?' she replied softly.

He looked at her angrily and then stormed out the door. She, after a pleading glance at me, ran out after him and I, well I, of course, went out after both of them. But we had not gone some three hundred feet down the road, when we were apprehended by cavalry. Tied to horses' tails, we were led into the Castle of Amboise and imprisoned.

They separated us, our captors, and incarcerated Madeleine with some women. I knew this because, as we were shoved along an underground passageway, she was the first to be dispatched into a cell. I had been holding her hand and something within me rejoiced to feel the softness of her palm even though I wished her miles away and safe in Normandy. A few times she grasped me hard as we tripped and stumbled in the dark passageway. Then we stopped and the guard, a rough, burly-looking fellow, opened a door and ordered her in, leering unpleasantly as he did so. Never will I forget how her little hand slipped out of mine – slipped away into the shadows. But I heard women's voices in the cell and thanked God for that. Yes, I thanked God. Strange how misfortune, war and affliction – how all these will take hold of a man and force him to his knees. And so it was with my heart, it was on its knees.

Charles had been quiet the whole time. All during our march to Amboise, as bushes scratched and branches hit us in the face, running and hobbling behind the horses, he had kept his mouth shut. Not lifting his head, he had only once made a sound. That was when we stumbled across the disembowelled corpses of three men whose lifeless bodies had been thrown onto a pile of stones. He had cursed. My brother, Charles, the Bible scholar, he had cursed. He whose close companion had been Jerome. The curse filled me with more dread than the dead bodies and I called out to him. But he would not look up. Madeleine likewise had been silent, but she, at least, looked at me from time to time. I could read fear mingled with fortitude in her eyes and I smiled reassuringly as best I could. And, as I said before, I prayed.

The cell into which Charles and I were thrown was at the end of a hall. It was a small cell and held no others. There was a window just above our heads – a window covered with a thick iron grille. Standing on our toes, we could just barely look out into the front courtyard of the castle. It was dusk, but there was much bustle and activity. An eerie busyness, for scaffolds were being prepared and I could see that the ground in front of me was red.

I cannot begin to tell you of the horrors which met our eyes day after day. It was put to me later by Jerome that perhaps I had done better not to look out into the courtyard, but to stay on my knees in the cell. Yet I must know whether Madeleine, whether she was with those condemned or not. Day and night the execution of the prisoners went on. Later I thought that God, in His great mercy, permitted us to be some of the first prisoners taken. That was providence indeed, for often I saw men and women marched up from beyond the castle confines only to be killed immediately. Perhaps our corridor, for some inexplicable reason, had been forgotten. The method of execution was diverse. Some were decapitated; others were hung; still others were rolled into sacks and drowned in the Loire. Most often the victims were slaughtered after dinner, for it was then that their deaths might amuse the royal court who were lodged above us. They watched from their dining room windows.

Each day the guard brought bread and water. He never spoke, but our provisions were ample and we marvelled that we were so provided for. At some point I mentioned to Charles that perhaps the man was an angel, but Charles only guffawed loudly, saying that angels were not likely to smell or swear, as he said the man did. I do not recall. But I do know the food was from God's hand.

For four dismal weeks the executions continued. I longed to send word to my father but dared not ask the guard to help for fear of giving him offense and so drawing attention to ourselves. At times the walls threatened to cave in on me and the continuous, odious, sweet smell of blood made our very bread taste like gall.

'Remember running bareheaded through the field?' I said to Charles.

He did not answer. He rarely spoke or answered. But I spoke on anyway, thinking that conversation, even a one-sided one, was good for both him and myself. It was somewhat like painting, these memories of which I spoke, and pictures emerged as I spoke of the very ordinary, mundane things – things such as walking about with a pruning hook on my shoulder and a billhook in my belt, making rounds of the fields to make sure the horses or pigs had not gotten in. And all the while I spoke I gazed outside and once saw a man dip his hands in the blood of one who had been executed just before him and heard him exclaim as he held up his hands to heaven.

'Lord, behold the blood of Thy children unjustly slain; Thou wilt avenge.'

I would have gone mad those hours in the cell had I not had the care of my brother. After we had been there a number of days, he would only eat if I fed him. The moments stretched long and longer and always I wondered about Madeleine. I also recalled vividly how last year at this time we had begun to dig around the surface roots of the orange and lemon trees and how we had grafted the figs and chestnuts. I could feel these actions in my hands and sometimes made motions, as if I were working alongside my father once more. And all the while victims died with the words of Psalms on their lips.

There came the day when I saw, with some measure of relief, that the royal court was departing Amboise. They rode out on white palfreys and handsome stallions, banners waving and swords glittering. They thought they rode bravely but the blood-soaked earth mocked them and the lifeless heads of countless victims spiked on poles next to the road grinned on them judgmentally. After they were gone, the stench of the corpses, especially when the wind over the Loire blew our way, became almost unbearable. Our guard, when he brought the rations, said nothing and we watched him depart in silence. Charles got up and walked over to the window. He stared at the gallows and mumbled something. I could not catch it and came closer. Then I saw that he was weeping. Putting my arm around his shoulder, I held him close and he sobbed like a baby. I was glad of it. This was better than the silence he had kept up for so long.

Two days later, our jailer spoke to us. Binding our hands with a thick rope, he ordered us to follow him. We looked at one another with apprehension and had no choice but to follow him down the corridor. I had not seen the executioner wield his axe since the court had departed from Amboise. But who was to say where we were being led? After a series of turns and twists, the jailer stopped in front of a cell door. Taking out his key, he opened it and harshly called out Madeleine's name. She appeared instantly and stepped into the corridor.

'Hussy!! Slut!!'

We heard the name-calling that followed her into the hall. She stumbled and fell on the cement floor. The jailer took hold of her waist, pulled her up, fondled her and whispered something into her ear. I wanted to hit the man, to lash out, but Charles restrained me.

'Not now,' he mouthed, 'Not now.'

The jailer continued to make free with Madeleine, who seemed like a straw doll in his hands. Her hair was matted and her eyes glazed. My hands itched to pulverize the man, to punch him so hard that he would fall down and never get up again. Something like a moan must have escaped my lips, for the jailer suddenly focused his attention on us.

'Well, and it isn't everyone here who can say they've lived through these past few weeks, is it, Maddie?'

Madeleine did not look at us but clenched her fists so that the knuckles showed white. I wanted to take those hands and hold them. I wanted to lead them away from here, from all the filth and degradation to which they had been subject.

'Well, Maddie, you can take your friends and go.'

We stared at him and he smiled, showing rotting teeth.

'Yes, go!! And that's what I've been promising Maddie these past few weeks – that as soon as the court left, I'd let her go and her brothers as well.'

He pulled Madeleine towards himself again and although she recoiled, she did not protest.

'Sorry to see you go though. And if I wasn't already married, I'd keep you here to be my wife, that's a sure thing.'

I fought the urge to vomit. The jailer reluctantly began his walk with us towards the end of the corridor. He took out his keys and opened several doors before we came to a final one which revealed a grass ledge of sorts. A path led away from it into the surrounding woods.

'Bear east and you'll be heading towards Normandy. That's where you're from, is that not so?'

He cut loose our ropes with his knife and as soon as I felt the cord slip free of my hand, I slugged him so hard we could hear the man's jaw break. I was about to hit him again, but Charles grabbed my arm.

'No, Gaspard! You'll have the whole garrison after us! Look, the man's out. We'll tie him up. There's the lad, just ease off.'

He spoke to me as I had spoken to him in the cell. The roles were reversed. Now I was the child. I looked on helplessly, paralysed with hatred, as Madeleine and Charles dragged the man back inside.

We bore east, as the guard had advised, ever looking back over our shoulders at Amboise. Soon it disappeared from sight and we heaved a sigh of relief. Charles had relapsed back into silence. Madeleine was also quiet and I could see that she struggled to keep up with us. She was a sad sight, poor girl! Thin, dirty and bruised, her dress in tatters, she seemed to have lost all the zeal she had displayed by coming here. I walked closer to her and tried to take her hand, even as I had done when we had been arrested so many weeks ago.

'Don't touch me!'

She whispered, but the whisper carried. It seemed as if the echo of her words rustled in the trees above us. I wondered that Charles did not try to comfort Madeleine. But then Charles, I told myself, had his own problems. For a while the beauty of the green forest enthralled me. It had been so long since I had touched a leaf. I reached out and pulled one off, studying its fine lines, its serrated edges, as we half-walked, half-ran in the direction of home. Birds sang around us and there arose in me such joy that I felt tears course down my face. And as they coursed down my face, I heard the psalms of the martyred men and women reverberate with the skylark.

We came home safely, thanks be to God. My father could not stop his marvelling for he had given us up for dead. There were such dreadful stories circulating, he said, and I was loath to tell him that they were true. The first night home, I went out to look at our fields and to count the stars. And who can do it?

Madeleine was received home as gladly as we had been. Her father was beside himself with joy and came to call on us again and again to express his gratitude. She had told him, he said, that she was going to visit a friend and he had not known that she was on her way to Amboise. If he had known, he would have forbidden it. He often looked at Charles as he spoke, but Charles avoided the man's gaze and would not be drawn into conversation. Later Charles told me that he was going south to join the Huguenot army.

'What about Madeleine?' I asked, perplexed that he should want to leave.

'What about her?'

'You wanted to wed her before all this,' I said, 'You were going to ask father ...'

'That was then,' he answered, interrupting me, 'and besides, she is spoiled goods now.'

I hit him hard, and as he smacked the floor, I remembered the jailer. I had wanted to kill the man. And would I now kill my brother? Evil will not be overcome by anger. It was Jerome who had spoken of this and I knew that he was right. Had I not seen hundreds die, stretching out their hands in love to those who had despitefully used them?

We did not see Madeleine for some months. I was fearful that she mourned the leaving of Charles and that she would forever live to think only of him. It was by chance that I heard the serving girls speak of her in such a way that I blushed. That evening I walked the fields and pondered. It was September and time to sow the wheat, the rye-wheat mixture and other grains. As well, we would soon harvest the grapes, knock down the walnuts and mow the late meadows. I stopped and dug my hand into the black earth. So God had fashioned man from the earth. I smelled the freshness of it. And He had breathed the breath of life into man. That is what Jerome said. And I knew it was true because I felt that life; I felt that breath; and I knew that I had been reborn.

I went to Sicort's the following day. Monsieur Sicort was cutting the twigs off the madder and looked surprised to see me.

'I've come for Madeleine,' I said, feeling rather sheepish.

'She's resting,' he answered rather curtly.

'Might I see her later then?'

He stopped his work and moved close to me.

'She's been through much, Gaspard. Why do you want to see her?'

He must have seen in my eyes why I wanted to see her and his own eyes registered even more surprise.

'She's in the kitchen, lad. Go on with you then.'

And there I was, my short, stocky body sweating with nervousness, lumbering through the grass as Monsieur Sicort's eyes followed me. One of the serving girls let me in, looking me over with great curiosity.

'Where is Mademoiselle Madeleine?'

'Here I am, Gaspard.'

Madeleine's voice rang through the kitchen. I asked the girl to leave and she did, although with difficulty. I walked on into the kitchen and found her at some embroidery. She was courteous but remained sitting, asking me if I would also sit. This I did and all the time I studied her face. She had regained her rosy cheeks and her hands, as they moved the needle, were strong and able.

'Do not stare so, Gaspard,' she said at length, 'it does not become you.'

I blushed and then, like my brother Charles, blurted out what I had been feeling for such a long time.

'I love you, Madeleine Sicort and I would ask your father's permission to wed you before winter.'

She dropped her embroidery on the floor and suddenly stood up.

'I think,' she began, 'you know not what most people are talking about in these parts.'

'Yes,' I answered, but she did not let me finish. She pushed out her stomach against the blue skirt she was wearing.

'Here I carry the jailer's child,' she said, 'and here is the ransom I paid for you and Charles. It was a dear price, but oh, I would ...'

She broke down and wept. I was by her side in an instant and put my arms around her shoulder but she pushed me away.

'No, Gaspard Palissy. You cannot ...'

Stricken to the soul, I let her go.

'You still love Charles.'

I had known it all along. My brother, the handsome, easy-going man of letters. She had lost her heart to him and would be constant.

'No,' she answered in a low voice, her eyes on the floor, 'I never loved Charles but as a brother. It was you I cared for always. I had perhaps hoped to make you a little jealous.'

She stopped and regarded me with a piteous glance before she went on.

'That is why I went with Charles ... to have you speak out, for you were always so ... so quiet. But I cannot let you marry me when I am thus stained. Always, always, people will point the finger at me. There she goes, they will say. There goes the slut who sold herself to the Papists.'

I was on my knees in an instant.

'Say not so, my love. Say not so.'

'Why not? It is true. Oh, Gaspard, I cannot be a true bride.'

'Yes, you can,' I answered, and with some difficulty because I was overcome with love – with love for her and for my Lord.

'How can you love me even now and why do you say this?'

Her voice broke and her tears fell on my neck.

'Because,' I answered, 'if my Lord took me while I was inconstant then why should I not take you as my sweet bride?'

They say it is given to each man to love once in his lifetime. I think that I would agree. And from that one all-encompassing love, they say, flow many other devotions. So, in any case, it was in my life – from one love, many. God chose me; Madeleine married me; and I was able to live a life which, if not always consistent with thankfulness, was a forgiven life.

And How Shall You Meet Your Maker?

And how shall your life continue?
Small the hour, still smaller second,
Looms the ticking clock within you
Counting off. You never reckon
That the minutes of the daylight,
That each pebble on your wayside,
Must be counted! Shall be counted!
Must be passed! Must be surmounted!
And – how shall your life continue?

And how shall your life move forward?
Each small thought and every action,
Every dead and untried effort
Will be brought before – no fraction
Of the time upon your life roll
Will be lessened from the life scroll.
Oh, how swift then! Yes, how swift then!
Will this timely pallor lift men.
And – how shall your life move forward?

And what shall you see awaking?
While the trifling, ordinary
Common day now mourns your taking –
Blackened, big obituary.
Friends behind their quiet hands share
Whispers while the casket stands there.
Does it matter? Does it matter?
As a droplet to the water.
And – what shall you see awaking?

Will you weep at all those faces
That among your lifetime blazing
Light up all your milestone places,
While Creator God is gazing?
Will there be a hopeless sorrow
That you thought not of tomorrow?
Will this happen? Has this happened?
Is your hold on heaven slackened?
Will you weep at all those faces?

And how shall you meet your Maker?
Bowing while the bell is tolling
And the mourners shed according,
Blinding tears to thunder rolling.
Will you wail for want of trying
As you hear His gavel crying
Justice on your life of darkness,
Pages, volumes of your starkness?
And – how shall you meet your Maker?

* * *

This is how your meet your Maker,
Christian child, with bleeding glances.
Fades the black-clad undertaker,
As the cross-stained Lamb advances.
Ah, His life your soul embraces,
Lifting far beyond these places.
It is done! There is no death now,
Condemnation has no breath now.
Hallelujah!! Praise the Lord!!

Christine Farenhorst

Meet the Author

Christine Praamsma was born on 10th September, 1948 in a small town in Holland. Her father, a pastor in the Gereformeerde Kerk, accepted a call to Canada in 1958.

Christine began telling stories before she could write. She used to draw pictures on her pillow before she went to sleep at night, relating the stories she drew to her teddy bear.

In 1969 she married her highschool sweetheart, Anco Farenhorst, a veterinarian. By God's grace they became the parents of five children. Grandchildren, as well, have been added to the grains of sand shown so long ago to Abraham.

Christine is also the author of two historical novels: *Wings Like a Dove*, and *A Cup of Cold Water*. As well, she has written several devotionals, other short story volumes, a collection of poetry, and has co-authored two church history text books for children.

A regular columnist for Reformed Perspective as well as a contributing writer for Christian Renewal, her first commitment is to be a godly Christian wife and mother. Her second is to use the talents that God has given her to the best of her ability and to His glory.

TIME · ETERNITY

AFTERWARDS
I KNEW
STORIES FROM THE FIRST
AND SECOND WORLD WARS

CHRISTINE FARENHORST

AND AFTERWARDS I KNEW
STORIES FROM THE FIRST AND SECOND WORLD WARS
CHRISTINE FARENHORST

ISBN: 978-1-84550-563-9

From the depths of history and the terrible days of the Great Wars we read stories of courage and danger but ultimately of faith, hope and love. A grandfather sits in front of a warm fire as the flames rekindle memories of times long gone – the next generation needs to know the truth. A table cloth and a large mischievous dog bring two women together from different sides of a bitter struggle.

Read these and other stories inspired by times past, but focussed on the truth of eternity.

HOW GOD STOPPED THE PIRATES
AND OTHER DEVOTIONAL STORIES
JOEL R. BEEKE & DIANA KLEYN

ISBN: 978-1-85792-816-7

As the pirates near the helpless ship they raise their grappling irons and prime their cannons for battle. The captain stands ready to defend his vessel and the lives of the people on board. The missionaries go to their cabins to pray. Can anyone stop these pirates? God can. There are lots of stories in this book. Read about the pirates, a burglar and a Russian servant girl as well as many other stories about the amazing things that missionaries get up to as well as how God can change lives.

Scriptural references are taken from the King James Version of the Bible and the questions are based on this. Suitable for 7-12 year olds.

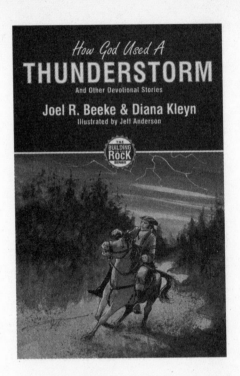

HOW GOD USED A THUNDERSTORM
AND OTHER DEVOTIONAL STORIES
JOEL R. BEEKE & DIANA KLEYN

ISBN: 978-1-85792-815-0

The mountains are dark and looming as the lightening splits across the sky. The forest offers shelter and in the distance the traveller spots a lamp. Rushing towards the door he doesn't realise that someone has planned this journey - there is a woman in the house who needs to hear about her loving Savior, Jesus Christ. God has sent the traveller to tell her about himself.

There are lots of stories in this book. Read about the thunderstorm, some hidden treasure and a Bible in a suitcase as well as many other stories about how we should live for God and read his word.

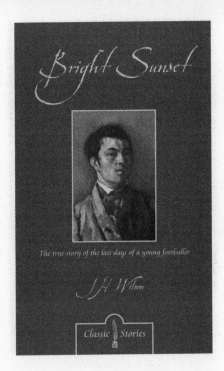

The true story of the last days of a young footballer

J H Wilson

Classic Stories

BRIGHT SUNSET
J. H. WILSON
ISBN: 978-1-84550-114-3

This is a true story! William Easton was enthusiastic about everything: school, friends, sports ... especially sports. Physically strong and robust, he was popular among all the other lads in his class at school. On the football field he was known both for his skill and his boundless energy. However, a tragic accident at sixteen years of age confined him to his bed and what everyone thought was just an accident turned out to be something far more serious and life threatening. William's life seems to be in ruins but he discovers, as do others, that in the middle of ruins - you can find treasure. This is the story of a great life given wholeheartedly to God.

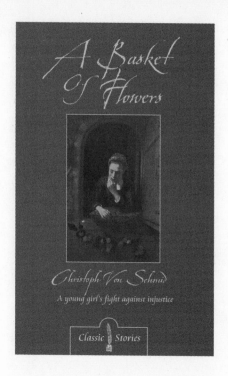

A BASKET OF FLOWERS
CHRISTOPH VON SCHMID

ISBN: 978-1-85792-525-8

Mary grows up sheltered and secure in a beautiful cottage with a loving father. She learns lessons about humility, purity and forgiveness under her father's watchful gaze. However, even though she loves God and obeys him this does not protect her ultimately from the envy and hatred of others. A beautiful gift and a jealous maid ensure that Mary and her father are imprisoned for a crime even though they are innocent. Eventually Mary is exiled from their home. In her troubles however God is a constant source of comfort to her and with an unexpected twist at the end of this story you can be sure that this book is a first rate read!

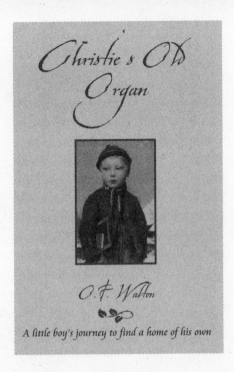

A little boy's journey to find a home of his own

CHRISTIE'S OLD ORGAN
O. F. WALTON
ISBN: 978-1-85792-523-4

Christie is homeless and on the streets of Victorian England - that's why he is overjoyed to be given a roof over his head by Old Treffy, the Organ Grinder. But Treffy is sick and Christie is worried about him. All that Treffy wants is to have peace in his heart and a home of his own. That is what Christie wants too. One day a girl called Mabel hears Christie's Old Organ playing outside her window. She becomes Christie's friend and tells him about another home you can go to if you love the Lord Jesus. Will Christie find this home? Will he ever have a family of his own? Let O. F. Walton tell you Christie's story.

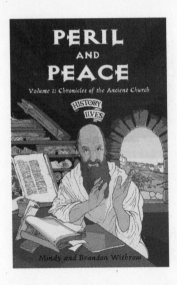

HISTORY LIVES: PERIL AND PEACE
CHRONICLES OF THE ANCIENT CHURCH
MINDY AND BRANDON WITHROW
978-1-84550-082-5

Read the stories of Paul, Polycarp, Justin, Origen, Cyprian, Constantine, Athanasius, Ambrose, Augustine, John Chrysostom, Jerome, Patrick, and Benedict – people from the early and ancient church, and discover the roots of Christianity. From the apostle Paul to Benedict you can discover how those in the early church still influence church today. Watch in amazement as people from different countries, cultures and times merge together to form the Christian church.

Learn from their mistakes and errors but more importantly learn from their strengths and gifts. Marvel at what God accomplished in such a short space of time.

Written in a modern and relaxed style this is a book that will introduce you to history without the tears and with all the wonder. There are longer chapters interspersed with short factual chapters. Extra features throughout this book look deeper into issues such as persecution; worship; creeds and councils and the formation of the Bible as well as a timeline.

HISTORY LIVES: MONKS AND MYSTICS
CHRONICLES OF THE MEDIEVAL CHURCH
MINDY AND BRANDON WITHROW
ISBN: 978-1-84550-083-2

Read the stories of Gregory the Great, Boniface, Charlemagne, Constantine Methodius, Vladimir, Anselm of Canterbury, Bernard of Clairvaux, Francis of Assisi, Thomas Aquinas, Catherine of Sienna, John Wyclif and John Hus. From Gregory I through to Wyclif and Hus you can discover about the crusades and the spread of Islam as well as the beginnings of universities and the Reformation.

As the church moves on through the centuries its people struggle against persecution and problems from inside and out. Learn from their mistakes and errors but more importantly learn from their amazing strengths and gifts. Marvel at God's wonderful care of his people - the church - the Christian church.

Written in a modern and relaxed style this is a book that will introduce you to history without the tears and with all the wonder. Extra features throughout this book include looking deeper into issues such as Islam; Division; the crusades; the first university; Creeds and Councils and the Renaissance.